THE HOMICIDAL HORSE

ALSO BY HUGH PENTECOST

Julian Quist Mystery Novels:

DEADLY TRAP
THE STEEL PALACE
DIE AFTER DARK
HONEYMOON WITH DEATH
THE JUDAS FREAK
THE BEAUTIFUL DEAD
THE CHAMPAGNE KILLER
DON'T DROP TOMORROW

Pierre Chambrun Mystery Novels:

RANDOM KILLER
DEATH AFTER BREAKFAST
THE FOURTEEN DILEMMA
TIME OF TERROR
BARGAIN WITH DEATH
WALKING DEAD MAN
BIRTHDAY, DEATHDAY
THE DEADLY JOKE
GIRL WATCHER'S FUNERAL
THE GILDED NIGHTMARE
THE GOLDEN TRAP
THE EVIL MEN DO
THE SHAPE OF FEAR
THE CANNIBAL WHO OVERATE

THE HOMICIDAL HORSE

Hugh Pentecost

A RED BADGE NOVEL OF SUSPENSE

DODD, MEAD & COMPANY
NEW YORK

Printed in the United States of America

1 2 3 4 5 6 7 8 9 10

Library of Congress Cataloging in Publication Data

Philips, Judson Pentecost, date
The homicidal horse.

(A Red badge novel of suspense)
I. Title.
PZ3.P5412Hl [PS3531.H442] 813'.5'2 79-20185
ISBN 0-396-07724-2

THE HOMICIDAL HORSE

PART ONE

1

Dan Garvey's love life was a source of affectionate but varied speculation in the offices of Julian Quist Associates, one of the top public relations firms in the country. In the very mod offices located in a finger of glass and steel pointing to the sky in the Grand Central Station area of New York, Garvey would have been surprised to know that the top associates down through the staff and the clerical force had a pool on who his date might be that night, and particularly that weekend. Garvey, handsome, dark, a former All-American and National Football League star running back until a knee injury cut his athletic career short, was suspected of having included quite a number of the staff among his conquests. But if that was true those ladies participated in the pool without any signs of jealousy or regrets. Garvey had promised nothing he hadn't delivered. He had never offered anything except the pleasure of the moment. If a lady dreamed of any kind of permanence with Dan Garvey, it was her own dream, not suggested or even vaguely hinted at by him. Garvey had played the field for years—until that summer.

For the last four years Garvey's almost total professional concerns had been with the great new Sports Complex built on Long Island. He had helped to raise money, to organize the operating machinery, to draw crowds to the indoor arena where major league hockey and basketball, indoor track and field events, dog shows, horse shows, and even political conventions had already become fixtures. The big dream was a new racetrack to take its place alongside Aqueduct and Belmont and Saratoga. Sports had been Garvey's whole life, and Julian Quist, the elegant man at the head of the firm, never ceased to congratulate himself that there was a Dan Garvey to promote the Island Complex. Nobody could have been better fitted for the job or could have handled it with more enthusiasm and skill.

That summer the pool on Garvey's love life was having a bleak stretch in which almost nobody won. The reason was the emergence on the scene of Ms. Judith Cameron. In the beginning nobody was certain whether the Ms. stood for Miss or Mrs. As far as the pool was concerned, Judith Cameron had broken the pattern on which the pool depended for its existence. Garvey was going steady!

Miss Gloria Chard, the glamorous receptionist in the office of Julian Quist Associates, believed by everyone to have almost certainly been a part of the Garvey scene, took it upon herself to find out what she could about Ms. Judith Cameron. Ms. Cameron was no young chick, Garvey's most frequent choice. She was a very wealthy widow of about thirty-five, lovely to look at, imbued with an easy, adult charm. Her chief interest in life was horses, and she owned a successful breeding farm in Kentucky. It was noted that Garvey had spent a couple of weekends at the farm. In fact, for the past two months Garvey had spent all his leisure time and much of his working time with Judith Cameron. She was vitally interested in the new racetrack on the Island, was in fact a substantial financial investor in its future.

"Count me out," Gloria Chard said one July morning when one of the girls came around to get her selection in the "Garvey pool." "Dan is hooked, and it's no longer a gamble. It looks like Ms. Cameron has our Daniel landed for keeps. I never enjoy betting on a sure thing."

But the very next day it was a different ball game.

About six o'clock in the morning Garvey was asleep—alone—in the small apartment he kept near the office in New York. His phone rang. A glance at his bedside clock told him it was an ungodly time for a call. When he answered he instantly recognized the voice of Vic Lorch, head of security at the Island Complex.

"Dan? Sorry to wake you, but we've got big trouble out here."

Garvey thought of fire. There were more than three hundred horses stabled at the track, in training, waiting for the green light to go.

"It's Ms. Cameron," Lorch said.

"*What?*"

"She's been stomped and kicked to death by a horse."

"Oh, dear God!" Garvey whispered, momentarily frozen where he lay.

The people at the Complex had evidently kept the lid on the story of what had happened to Judith. Garvey kept turning the radio dial on the dash of his Jaguar as he speeded out along the thruway, but he got no clue. The story hadn't broken.

"She can't be dead!" he'd said on the phone to Vic Lorch.

"Sorry, Dan."

He'd called the garage to get his car out, thrown on clothes, set out for the Complex. It just couldn't be. He had left her a little before midnight at her rented house on the

Island. He hadn't spent the night, though invited, because he had an early morning business appointment in the city and needed to see Julian Quist first. It was a tender, relaxed parting. Very much sooner than anyone suspected, there were going to be no partings. Gloria Chard was right. Garvey was landed for keeps. In August Judith would take her stable of horses north to Saratoga for the month of racing, a meeting no genuine horseman would miss. After that she and Garvey would slip away to be married, and that would be that.

She's been stomped and kicked to death by a horse. Lorch's voice, heard only minutes ago, took on the quality of some ghoulish monster in a horror film as Garvey listened to the words again in his memory. Not possible! Just not possible! Judith, so very feminine, so gracious, so relaxed, so lovely, had another side where she functioned with expert skills. She had been brought up with horses by her millionaire father. Garvey impressed, had watched her work with horses. She was patient yet insistent. The horse she was schooling could delay and delay doing what she was demanding, but in the end he must obey. She treated her horses with affection, but she was always on guard against some unexpected action.

They had laughed about it.

"You should never let a man who thinks about you seriously watch you work a horse," he'd told her, early on.

"Men and horses are two very different animals," she'd said, smiling. "Have you ever noticed me trying to lead you on the dance floor?"

Nor in lovemaking, he thought. He was allowed to lead, and yet the climaxes were a mutual accomplishment, beyond belief. Somehow they were meant for each other, and by some lucky miracle they had found each other.

. . . *Stomped and kicked to death by a horse*!

The parking lot at the Complex was a vast, deserted concrete plateau as Garvey raced across it toward the stable area—Shed Row. Horses were out on the track, being taken through their paces by exercise boys. Out of key with the normal morning scene was the presence of several police cars and a knot of people who didn't belong there. Garvey, waved to a halt by a state trooper, scrambled out of his car. Coming toward him from the crowd of people was Vic Lorch. Lorch was a big man, six feet two or three, wearing blue jeans, cowboy boots, and a leather vest over a blue-and-white checkered shirt. He was hatless, his thick mat of dark hair as always in disorder. He had bright grey eyes that were narrowed this morning against some kind of pain.

Garvey started to barge past his friend as though he hadn't seen him. Lorch's big hands reached out and took him by the shoulders, stopping him.

"Easy, Dan," he said.

"Where is she?" Garvey asked, his voice unsteady.

"They've taken her away."

"Where?"

"State Police morgue, I think, for an autopsy."

"They're not going to cut her up!" Garvey said, trying to wrench free.

"It doesn't matter much, Dan," Lorch said. "She was terribly mangled by the horse."

"What horse?" An insane need for revenge was burning inside Garvey's skull. He looked down to the far end of Shed Row, past the curious heads of scores of horses peering over the tops of the half-doors to their box stalls. One of them was a murderer, Garvey thought, still not rational.

"Not one of hers," Lorch said, fingers biting into the flesh of Garvey's shoulders. "In a way, not one of hers. Not in her stable area. A three-year-old named King Lear who won a stake race at Aqueduct yesterday. He was being stabled here, trucked over to the Big A to run."

"What do you mean, 'in a way not one of hers'?"

"She bred him at her farm. Sold him at the Saratoga yearling sales to Jerry Carpenter two summers ago. I guess she didn't think the King had much of a future. Neither did the bettors. He paid off at about sixty-to-one yesterday. Someone made a killing."

Garvey made a violent effort and broke away from his friend. He ran down between the stalls on Shed Row. He knew where the Carpenter horses were stabled—at the far end of the row and at right angles in the T-shaped area. But he didn't have to hunt for King Lear's stall. Two state troopers were standing outside it. They saw him coming and blocked his way. Held by them, he looked past them into the stall. A bay colt lay flat in the straw, which was spattered with what looked like quarts of blood. The colt was obviously dead.

A heavy hand rested on Garvey's shoulder. Vic Lorch had caught up with him. He turned Garvey away.

"Ben Diamond, a stable hand for Carpenter, heard her screaming," Lorch said. "He ran down here from the tack room where he was making coffee for himself. Ms. Cameron was down in the straw, with the horse rearing up and coming down on her with his iron-shod hooves. Ben tried to go in and grab him, but the horse was wild. Ben ran back to the tack room and got a handgun they keep there. He came back and shot the horse. Too late. Ms. Cameron's head had been smashed in like a rotten pumpkin."

"Oh, Jesus!" Garvey said.

Suddenly he was crying like a child, his face buried against Vic Lorch's shoulder.

*

You think you have some kind of a secret that you've kept private, and then something unexpected happens, and it turns out that the whole world knows it. Garvey's friendship with Judith Cameron had not been a secret. They had been seen together constantly at the Complex. It was known that he visited her frequently at her rented house a few miles farther out on the Island. She went to the city to do a little fancy pub-crawling with him now and then. They weren't much on late nights out because Judith wasn't just the owner of horses, she took an active part in supervising and training them. This meant that her schedule took her to Shed Row and the exercise track in the very early hours of every morning. You could find her at about 5 A.M. having a cup of coffee and juice at the short-order bar at the mouth of Shed Row. Garvey was known to be a man who played the field. The secret they thought they had kept was that their relationship wasn't just a sex frolic. They were deeply in love, and after Saratoga in August, they were to marry.

On the morning Judith Cameron died, it seemed that everyone who knew them knew how much more their relationship was than fun and games. The hardest thing for Garvey to take was the sympathy and concern from all kinds of people he never dreamed gave a damn for him or his happiness. It was like living through the tragedy over and over, every twenty minutes. He finally retired to his office in the Arena Building of the Complex to be alone and to try to put together the shattered pieces of his life. There was no one to be angry at—except a dead horse. It was just one of those things. An awful thing.

Perhaps the closest person to Garvey in the world, except the woman he had just lost, was Julian Quist, the man he worked for and with. Quist had picked Garvey up after his football career was ended, brought him into his public relations firm, eventually made him a partner, an associate.

Temperamentally these two friends were very different. Garvey was dark, intense, introverted, private; Quist was public glamour. He was a tall, slender, graceful man, his blond hair worn long, his profile carved like a piece of Greek sculpture. He was fond of clothes, very mod clothes, and in the dressing room of his Beekman Place duplex there were closets full of them. In the nightspots around town he was a familiar and much admired figure, always accompanied by the beautiful Lydia Morton, who made no bones of the fact that she shared the Beekman Place duplex with Quist, even though she kept a small apartment of her own a few blocks away. A researcher, gifted writer and designer, she was one of the associates in Julian Quist Associates. Garvey had spotted Lydia in his first days of working for Quist, and decided "she's for me." He very quickly discovered that Lydia was for no one but Julian, and would never be for anyone but Julian. He knew envy for the first time in his life, not so much because he couldn't have Lydia, but because her relationship with Quist was so perfect. He didn't believe he could ever have anything like that for himself. Then he had found Judith. And now he had lost her.

The door to Garvey's office in the Arena Building opened and Quist stood there. He was wearing a pink linen suit and a navy blue sports shirt. He looked at Garvey, who was sitting at his desk, face buried in his hands. Quist's blue eyes had darkened with pity for his friend. Garvey looked up, saw Quist, and turned away, convulsed again by his grief and shock.

Quist went to the windows and looked out over the vast expanse of the Complex—the restaurants, the parking lot, the distant stables. Garvey was responsible for most of what he saw. Garvey had raised most of the money for it, had engaged the architects who first put the dream on paper, had supervised its building, had set it in motion. It was a monument to a hard-driving, determined, dedicated man.

Quist lit a thin black cigar, which he had extracted from a leather case. Those cigars were specially made for him.

"You shouldn't be sitting here, slopping over," Quist said, in a very casual, conversational tone.

"I know," Garvey said. "Do you know that less than twelve hours ago I was holding her in my arms?"

"You spent the evening with her?"

"The early part. I went back into town because I was supposed to meet you this morning before going to the Rockledge Foundation about special funds."

"The reason I say you shouldn't be here slopping over," Quist said, "is because I don't buy it."

"Don't buy what?"

"I don't think it was an accident, Dan. I think your lady was murdered."

Garvey was on his feet. "What the hell are you talking about?"

"I think it's time you came back into the world and listened to what there is to hear," Quist said.

2

Garvey, standing rigid, faced his friend. "Truth or therapy?" he asked, sounding almost hostile. "Because I'm not interested in prescriptions for ways to stop feeling sorry for myself. I am sorry for myself!"

"I understand that," Quist said. He perched on the edge of Garvey's desk, dangling one pink-trousered leg. "Do you know how long you've been in this office by yourself?"

"I suppose an hour."

"More," Quist said. He glanced at his gold wristwatch. "It's almost noon. I stayed away from you as long as I could, Dan. Now it's time for you to blow your nose, wipe your eyes, and start taking a look at things."

"I loved her, Julian."

"I know." Quist tipped the ash from his cigar into the glass tray on the desk. "But I think there is an account to settle for Judith, Dan. And I suspect that you—with whatever help I can give you—are the only person genuinely interested in settling it."

"I asked you once what the hell are you talking about?" Garvey said.

"A preliminary report from the medical examiner has just been delivered to Captain Mowery of the State Police," Quist said. "He's in charge of the case, if you didn't know. Vic Lorch told me, just before I came in here, what's in that report."

"And?"

"There was a bullet in Judith's brain," Quist said. "The medical examiner can't make a certain determination whether it lodged there before or after the horse crushed her skull to a pulp. If it was before, it could have caused her death. If it was after King Lear destroyed her—" Quist shrugged.

"But why, in God's name—?"

"Oh, there's an explanation," Quist said. "You see, the bullet in Judith's head matches, ballistically, the two bullets that Ben Diamond, the stable hand, fired into the head of King Lear. Same gun. I think you should hear Ben Diamond's story from him."

"What does he say?"

"It's straight enough," Quist said, his eyes narrowed against the smoke from his cigar. "Diamond relieves the night watchman in that section of Shed Row about five o'clock. He checked out the horses in his care. He works for Jerry Carpenter, and Carpenter has nine horses stabled in that section. He found everything okay and went to the tack room to make himself some coffee. The coffee was just about ready when he heard Judith screaming. He ran out into the alley between the rows of stalls, not certain where the sound came from. Horses were excited up and down the alley, stirring nervously in their stalls. He could hear the thrashing and kicking somewhere down the line. He wasn't sure, for a moment, whether the screams he'd heard were human, as he'd first thought. What he heard now was coming from an enraged animal.

"He ran down the row of stalls, looking into each one. It

was King Lear, yesterday's stake winner, who was rearing, and plunging, and screaming. He saw Judith, lying in the straw, her head crushed. The horse wasn't finished with her. He was rearing up and coming down on her with his front feet. Diamond knows horses. He opened the lower half of the stall door and started in. The horse, lathered with sweat, eyes wild, turned his attention to Diamond. Diamond ran for his life, slamming the stall door closed behind him. He knew there was a gun in the tack room. It's kept there to deal with night prowlers, vandals. He got the gun and went back to King Lear's stall. The horse was at work on Judith again."

"Oh, God!" Garvey said.

"Diamond says he didn't hesitate. He opened fire on the horse. The gun is a six-shot revolver. There are two unfired bullets in the chamber now, two in King Lear's head, one in a wooden beam at the rear of the stall—and one in Judith's head. Diamond doesn't remember how many shots he fired. He says he just kept pulling the trigger till the horse went down. But it seems he fired four shots. One of them went wild and struck the already dead Judith."

"What's wrong with the story?" Garvey asked when Quist didn't go on.

"We've worked together for what—ten years now, Dan? We've encountered some violences in our time. I'm a hunch man. I have some kind of cockeyed instinct for a lie. I don't think Diamond is telling the truth. Mind you, I haven't seen him yet or talked to him. I'm not reacting to him as a man. I just don't believe the story."

"Why, for God sake?"

"Some questions I haven't had a chance to ask, so I don't have answers," Quist said. "But what was Judith doing in Jerry Carpenter's section of Shed Row at five o'clock in the morning in a stall with one of Carpenter's horses?"

"She could have been walking that way toward her own section," Garvey said. "She saw something wrong with the horse and went in to help it. Horses have been her life. She'd have had no fear."

"No," Quist said.

"Why not?"

"I don't know, but no," Quist said. "She knew horses so well. If she saw that King Lear had gone berserk for some reason, she wouldn't have walked into his stall."

"She was brave," Garvey said. "She didn't know the meaning of fear."

"Not crazy brave," Quist said. "The lion tamer knows when it's too dangerous to go into the lion's cage." His mouth moved in a wry smile. "Strange, isn't it? The original King Lear went mad. This horse went mad for some reason. You suppose winning that stake race yesterday was too much for him? He paid sixty-to-one, I understand."

"King Lear." Garvey said. "She raised him at Cameron Farms. She bred him. Jerry Carpenter bought him at the yearling sales in Saratoga a couple of years back. She spoke about it last night."

Quist sat very still on the edge of the desk.

"She didn't think this colt had much promise," Garvey said. "She thought Carpenter had been something of a sucker to buy him. She was astonished to hear about yesterday's stake race. Set a new track record for a mile and a quarter. 'I'd have bet an arm and a leg he'd never amount to anything,' she told me—last night."

"So she was wrong," Quist said.

"But that explains it, doesn't it?" Garvey asked. "She goes to work this morning by way of Carpenter's stable area to have a look at the colt she bred and raised—who'd just won a big one. The horse would be like her child to her, you know?"

Quist was silent for a moment. "I don't buy that either," he said.

Julian Quist's career as a public relations expert brought him into contact with the top people in many segments of society. The heads of many big multinational corporations—the big five hundred—were his clients; film and stage stars; politicians running for office. All of them used Quist's talents to create a public image that, more often than not, wasn't a true picture of the real person. Quist remembered his father, long ago, talking about his service in the Army. "I thought I was fighting to save the world for democracy," the elder Quist said, "but I found out I was fighting to save the oil companies." False fronts and false faces were the public relations expert's job to create.

As a result, in his private life Quist tended to enjoy the company of "characters"—a colorful Irish bartender in a Third Avenue saloon, a taxi driver who knew the truth about all the city scandals, a stage doorman who knew that the romantic leading man is gay and could name his boyfriends. Most were people who apply a kind of sardonic humor to the real truth about almost anything.

Among Quist's friends in this offbeat world was one Willie "Slick" Jacobs. Willie's world was horse racing. He spent his life at Belmont, at Aqueduct, at Saratoga, with an occasional trip to Hialeah in the winter and, of course, to the Derby in Kentucky and the Preakness in Maryland in the spring. Willie could have been a character invented by Damon Runyon or the late Joe Palmer, greatest of all the racetrack writers of our time. Quist discovered, along the way, that a great deal of Willie's colorful conversation was right out of Joe Palmer's collected columns.

Willie had a credo about horse racing that he had lifted almost word for word from Joe Palmer. In that one instance he gave credit where credit was due.

"Like Joe Palmer used to say," Willie would say, "I am no noted lover of the horse, but of a way of life of which the horse was once, and in a few favored places still is, a symbol—a way of charm and ease and grace and leisure. Joe Palmer never called it the sport of kings. It is a sport of ladies and gentlemen and cheerful brigands and small, skillful boys. That was good enough for Joe Palmer and it's good enough for me." Willie would shake his head. "Any man who would try to change that way of life would stir champagne." Another Palmerism for which Willie didn't always give credit.

Willie could tell you all there was to know about the hangers-on around the racetracks—the experts at the fix, the sellers of the Brooklyn Bridge, the stealers of the widow's mite, the morning clockers, the Shed Row experts who purveyed esoteric information straight from the horse's mouth, about who would win the feature race on any given day. "Tout" is a more familiar name for them.

Willie, by what Quist considered a piece of luck, was at the Complex on the morning of Judith Cameron's death. Quist had persuaded Garvey to try to get Ben Diamond, the stable hand who had shot King Lear, to tell his story again to someone who wasn't a cop. Quist sat in the shade of an ancient oak tree, fifty yards from Shed Row. Squatting beside him, chewing on a straw, was the small, ferret-faced, bright-eyed Willie Jacobs.

"Too damned bad. Great lady," Willie said. "One of the very few people who still knew what the world of racing is supposed to be."

"You knew her?"

"I know everyone who's of any consequence in this cock-eyed world," Willie said.

Quist knew Willie meant the world of horse racing. Any other worlds didn't exist for Willie. Even as he talked, his eyes roamed the Shed Row area, watching a horse being cooled out by a small boy, watching the little groups of twos and threes stopping to gossip. Judith Cameron had provided them with more than the daily hearsay scandal this day.

"How does it sit with you, Willie?" Quist said.

Willie smiled his crooked smile. "If I wanted to con you for a fast loan, I'd say it doesn't sit well with me," Willie said. "Because it obviously doesn't sit well with you. Why doesn't it?"

Quist reached down into the grass and pulled up what he hoped was a four-leaf clover. It wasn't. "I've got a machine inside me, Willie," he said, "that tells me if a man is lying when a situation doesn't ring true. My machine tells me something stinks about the story we've heard so far."

Willie's bright little eyes fixed on Quist's face. "Would your machine tell you whether the odds on a horse in the fourth were too long? If it would, you could close up your business and become a millionaire just sitting out here in the sun."

"Like sixty-to-one?" Quist asked.

"So you're at least at square one," Willie said. "King Lear had no more right to win that stake race yesterday than I would, pulling a milk wagon behind me."

"Mrs. Cameron thought that. She told Garvey last night."

"Like I always thought, bright lady," Willie said.

"Courtesies of the track," Quist said. "Does one owner walk down Shed Row and go into the stall of another owner's horse without asking permission?"

"Your machine's workin' up a storm, friend," Willie said. "You wouldn't go near a horse—nearer than the stall door to pat his nose if it was sticking out—unless the owner or the trainer or the groom assigned to him gave you the word. The woods are full of people who don't have the right kind of interest in an animal."

"But if Judith walked by to have a look at this horse—a horse she bred and raised, a horse that won a stake race yesterday—and saw he was in trouble—?"

"What kind of trouble?"

"Down. Tangled up in some way."

"She'd walk four stalls down the line to the tack room, where there's always someone if he isn't out front in the alley."

"If I saw a man down in the street and I suspected a heart attack," Quist said, "I wouldn't stop to ask permission to help him."

Willie chewed on his straw thoughtfully. "How to put it to you, man," he said. "You don't give a horse mouth-to-mouth, you know? Mrs. Cameron, who knew all the niceties, would just get help where she knew it would be—if she saw the horse in trouble."

"But she did go into the stall, and the horse went berserk and attacked her."

"Your machine is starting not to work," Willie said, and looked away at some cooling horses.

"Why do you say that?"

"You said something stinks about the story we've heard. For my money that's where the stink starts—where she walked into the stall and the horse went crazy."

"Explain," Quist said.

"Mrs. Cameron knew horses like you know people," Willie said. "She grew up with them. So let's say she had some reason to want to look at King Lear. She walks along Shed Row till she comes to his stall. She looks in and there he is. She speaks to him. People who love animals have a way of talking to animals, a tone of voice, a something. If the horse is okay he will come over to the half-door and stick his head out. If the horse is okay she will pet him, talk to him. But if the horse is strung-up, crazy, Mrs. Cameron would know in an instant. Nothing in the world would persuade her to go into the stall. She was too wise, too savvy."

"But she did go in. She was there. Maybe something happened to the horse after she went in. Maybe he was stung by a bee. Something we can't explain that frightened him."

Willie picked up a pebble in the grass and tossed it away, aimlessly. "Would you buy the idea that that's what we're supposed to think?" he asked.

Quist felt a strange, prickling sensation at the back of his neck. "Keep talking, Willie,"

"Dreams," Willie said. "Maybe you'd call 'em nightmares. But let's imagine. Ben Diamond hears screaming. He runs down the alley and sees King Lear, gone crazy, stomping on the lady in the straw. He goes into the stall, he says, to try to grab the horse by the halter and is attacked. He runs for his life, gets the gun in the tack room, comes back and shoots at a rearing, plunging horse. He hits him in the head, which would be high above his own head. He misses with one shot that winds up in the stall wall, up high. But a fourth shot that misses winds up in the head of a lady who is lying on the stall floor in the straw." Willie sighed. "Now what does your machine tell you?"

"The horse lunged at him, deflecting his aim," Quist said.

"You think Ben Diamond went into the stall with that gun, a horse striking out at him with iron hooves? I don't know what your machine tells you, friend, but I say never. I say he stays outside the stall door and fires from there. Once he decides to kill the horse he doesn't have to go in and try to handle him. Ben Diamond likes living as much as the next guy, I imagine," Willie said. "So," and his eyes were narrow slits, "he fires three shots at the horse, hitting with two, and one shot at the lady who was on a totally different aim line."

"Why?" Quist asked.

"Would you buy that he didn't want her to come to and tell us what really happened? Would you buy that she never went into that stall under her own power, that she was shot outside the stall and dumped in there, the horse stirred up by inflicting some kind of pain on him? You pays your money and you takes your choice." Willie found another pebble and tossed it away.

"You think it was one of those ways?" Quist asked quietly.

"Let me ask how your machine reacts to something else," Willie said. "You're not a horse racing man, friend, but surely you must realize when a sixty-to-one shot wins a stake race more than one eyebrow is going to rise up."

"You're suggesting a fix?" Quist asked.

"This horse—this King Lear—not only won a stake race at sixty-to-one, he set a new track record for a mile and a quarter," Willie said. "So nobody held back, or pulled up, or rode out. At that pace King Lear would have run that field into the ground the best day they ever saw. So the race wasn't fixed out on the track."

"How then? You're suggesting somebody made a killing on that race?"

Willie nodded. "A few hundred bucks, only, bet at the track. God knows how much at the off-track betting parlors around the country. The first question any horseman would ask is—drugs? Well, the answer is no. Every horse that finishes in the money is given a urinalysis after each race. King Lear passed the test or they wouldn't have paid off on him."

"So he had an unexpectedly good day," Quist said.

"How are the odds arrived at?" Willie said. "This isn't

1910 when the individual bookmakers set their own odds. Today the totalizator right out there in plain view sets the odds, according to the money bet at the windows. The racing fans themselves set the odds by where they put their money. How do they decide? They read the yellow sheet, the pink sheet, or whatever tout sheet they follow. What is the horse's past record? King Lear had no record of ever—*ever*, mind you—finishing in the money, first, second, or third. But he set a track record yesterday. So only a few very wise guys put any dough on him—those few and a couple of crackpots who always bet on the long shot."

"What are you getting at, Willie?" Quist asked, beginning to know the answer before he got it.

"King Lear's past record doesn't account for it," Willie said. "It wasn't drugs. So why do you think I'm here this morning instead of back at Aqueduct where the action is? It's to ask a question, friend—a question a lot of smart horsemen may be asking today. Was King Lear really King Lear?"

"A ringer," Quist said.

"It happened a year ago at Aqueduct," Willie said. "A horse died, a no-account horse. Some smart guys announced that it was a good horse that had died, and then ran that good horse under the no-account's name. Over a hundred and fifty years of racing, that's been tried enough times to make a shrewd horseman wonder."

"So King Lear wasn't King Lear," Quist said.

"Just to suppose," Willie said. "I say smart horsemen may have asked themselves that question. Your Mrs. Cameron was a very smart horseman—horsewoman. Not only that, she bred and raised King Lear. There could be something about the colt she would know, some obscure marking, some old scar. So—" and Willie shrugged, "—something for the guessing game. Would that explain why she might have broken the rules of stable etiquette and gone into the stall with that colt without asking permission? Maybe she could tell if King Lear was really King Lear. Somebody found her there trying to make sure."

"Ben Diamond!" Quist said.

"Maybe not," Willie said. "But if King Lear was a ringer, if there had been a switch, he'd almost certainly have to be in on it. Someone else sees the lady there, gets the gun from the tack room, shoots her, replaces the gun. Then Diamond stages the cover-up, barges down the Shed Row alley, shoots the horse."

"But the horse had gone berserk."

"Someone inflicted some kind of unendurable pain on him," Willie said. He stood up, straightening stiffened knee joints. "So endeth the first lesson."

As head of security at the Island Complex, Vic Lorch had a variety of responsibilities. He had a force of about twenty men, whom he'd been allowed to select for himself. Their duty was to protect the plant against vandalism, to keep the place clear of pickpockets, con men, and accomplished swindlers bent on victimizing the public. Vic Lorch's men moved around quietly in the crowds when an event was in progress, watching, looking for a familiar, crooked face. In addition to this specialized group of Lorch's, there was an army of ushers and special cops who could be called on to maintain order if there was any kind of customer flare-up.

Vic Lorch, when there was no general public, moved around the plant in his blue jeans, cowboy boots, leather vest, and gaudy sports shirts. You could pick him out at a distance because of his matted dark hair. When there were paying customers, Lorch transformed himself into a Madison Avenue executive—dark suit, white shirt, conservative tie..

It was early afternoon, and the Complex was still alive with state troopers, trying to clean up the Cameron tragedy.

"Paul Mowery's going crazy trying not to hear whispers," Vic Lorch told Quist. The two men were sitting in Lorch's small office in the basement of the Arena.

"Captain Mowery is in charge of the local troop?" Quist asked.

"Yeah. Not a homicide man himself, but he has people, experts. It all looked so simple at five o'clock this morning, Mr. Quist. Lady done to death by a homicidal horse. Too many whispers now to let it lie there."

"You heard the ringer theory?"

Lorch nodded. "Top of the list by now," he said.

"Your opinion?" Quist asked.

"Could be," Lorch said. "My opinion isn't solid yet. But let me point something out to you, Mr. Quist. The racing people have their own special security, their own special cops. They rent space from the Complex, but they take care of themselves. My boys and I aren't in the act down there at Shed Row at all. Like you or anyone else hanging around here today, we hear the talk, but it's not our business. Nor has Mowery asked us to take a hand."

"But I know you too well to think you're just sitting around whistling 'Dixie,' " Quist said.

Lorch grinned. "I'm like a crossword puzzle nut," he said. "I see one, I try to solve it."

"So catch me up with you."

Lorch fished a cigarette out of his shirt pocket and lit it. "You know Jerry Carpenter, who owns the horse?" he asked.

"Just to say hello. I've seen him around a couple of nightspots in the city, always with some beautiful doll," Quist said.

"You have to begin with him," Lorch said. "He owns the

horse. Now Jerry Carpenter is so rich, Mr. Quist, it hurts. A house here on the Island, another in Florida, a farm in Kentucky, a yacht, and he owns a piece of a professional football team. He leaks money. He is the last man in the world who would need to fix a horse race in order to raise some quick cash. So right away he is a kind of roadblock to the theory of a ringer or any other kind of fix."

"But—"

"Carpenter buys a colt, King Lear, from Mrs. Cameron at the yearling sales in Kentucky or Saratoga or someplace two years back. Mrs. Cameron kids him about it because she tells him in advance this particular colt has no future. But what the hell, he's got the dough to throw around. Probably give him a kick to be right and have a real expert like Mrs. Cameron be wrong. So they try King Lear as a two-year-old in Florida. He's got lead in his feet. He shows nothing. He shows nothing as a three-year-old. Never places in any race he starts.

"Now Carpenter has some oil interests in South America. He decides to spend some time down there, and he ships some of his lesser horses to Buenos Aires for the season there, among them King Lear. Down there the horse still looks like a candidate for the dog-food factory."

"Our Mr. Carpenter doesn't give up easily," Quist said.

Lorch shrugged. "There are real horsemen and there are people who own horses," he said. "Maybe Carpenter just didn't want to be proved wrong about the colt. Maybe he forgot all about him and he was just a name on a list of names. You'd think Hank Benson, his trainer, one of the best, would have advised him to stop spending money for oats for King Lear. Anyway, three days ago the Carpenter horses are shipped back from South America. Most of the good ones are stabled at Aqueduct. There are nine here. When one of them is entered in a race, he's trucked over to

Aqueduct and brought back afterward. King Lear was never entered in anything until yesterday. Yesterday he becomes some kind of spectacular speed horse and sets a new track record."

"A colt could mature," Quist said.

"Could," Lorch agreed. "But there are a lot of smart guys around racing whose lives are devoted to making sure no one springs a surprise. They're called clockers. You see them hanging over the rail at all the early morning workouts, timing, timing, timing. The word is that King Lear wasn't given much work and that nobody ever saw him show anything worth clocking. He was, until yesterday, a dog."

"But yesterday he's blazing hot."

"Right."

"And today he's a killer?"

"Yes. But there is still one thing that makes you ask questions. How could a man, aiming a gun at a horse that's rearing up over his head, get off a shot that's so wild it hits a lady lying in the straw at his feet?"

"Garvey's talking to Ben Diamond," Quist said.

"Oh, good old Ben will have a believable explanation," Lorch said. "Wouldn't you if you were Ben?"

"Guilty or innocent?"

"If you were guilty, of course you'd have an explanation," Lorch said. "If you were innocent, your explanation, no matter how farfetched, would eventually stand up because it would be the truth."

Quist moved restlessly across the office to a small window overlooking the parking lot. "The person I guess I should talk to is Hank Benson, the trainer."

"You want some advice, Mr. Quist?" Lorch asked.

Quist turned back from the window. "That's why I'm here, Vic."

"The question-and-answer approach isn't going to get you

anything—but answers," Lorch said. "Prepared answers, answers they can't wait to give you. There are a whole hatful of people I wouldn't question until I had some ammunition. People like Jerry Carpenter, King Lear's owner; Hank Benson, his trainer; Ed Smythe, Carpenter's head groom; Ben Diamond, who shot the horse and the lady; Donny Coburn, King Lear's jockey; Clem Maguire, Carpenter's veterinarian. If it was a fix or a rig, they'll all have answers."

"So what would you do?"

"I'd become all ears," Lorch said. "And I'd get other ears to listen for me. My boys will listen for you, Mr. Quist. They'd be listening anyhow. And didn't I see you talking to Slick Jacobs awhile back?"

"Willie's an old friend," Quist said.

"He hears more than anybody," Lorch said. He laughed. "Willie even hears what the horses say to each other."

"It is murder, isn't it, Vic?"

Lorch crushed out his cigarette. "If that horse was a ringer, Mrs. Judith Cameron was someone who might have established it beyond question. So I say, if the horse was a ringer then it was murder—or could have been murder—or might have been murder."

3

The talk around Shed Row at the Island Complex didn't have much to do with the questions Quist and Garvey had been asking. Murder had not popped into the mind of the hundreds of people who moved in and out of the stable area. People have been kicked to death in stables enough times down through the years to make the idea acceptable. Quist and Garvey, who did not live with horses, assumed Judith Cameron was too smart a horsewoman to have let herself into a stall with a dangerous animal. Horse people were more cynical. It is more often the best steeplechase jockey who gets thrown and breaks his neck because he takes risks a lesser rider wouldn't take. Most people around Shed Row who knew the background thought it was perfectly normal for Judith to have stopped by to have a look at the colt she'd bred and raised after he'd just won a big one, setting a track record. They didn't question the "etiquette" of her letting herself into the stall of a horse belonging to someone else. Maybe they or the next guy wouldn't do it, but Judith Cameron and Jerry Carpenter were old friends with adjoining farms in Kentucky. This particular horse had been a joke between them. It seemed a perfectly permissible action on Judith's part. She knew the colt, would have had a normal curiosity about how he'd come out of his record-breaking win—in sound condition? Something had turned a normally lazy colt into a raging killer. There was some curiosity about what that "something" could have been, but among high-strung thoroughbreds sudden hysteria wasn't unheard of.

What Shed Row *was* talking about was the unexpected win by King Lear, a sixty-to-one shot. Somebody had made a killing—if somebody could have known it was going to happen. A thousand dollars, spread around in hundred-dollar bets, would have returned sixty thousand dollars.

What would make such a windfall a crime? If the horse was a ringer it would be a crime. The use of illegal stimulants would make it a crime, but the tests after the race seemed to rule that out. The Carpenter stable could have staged a con game that *wouldn't* have been a crime. The shrewd rail-birds, the clockers, had watched King Lear work and reported the colt had shown nothing. That could have been planned, staged. There is no law that says you must make your colt show his best for the morning clockers. Their reports, seeping out to the bettors, help determine the odds. But you're not *required* to reveal anything in your workouts.

"The colt was a late bloomer," some wise guy suggested. "He showed nothing as a two-year-old and nothing early in his three-year-old season. They take him to South America, where he begins to come alive. By the time they're ready to bring him back to the States they know they've got something. They keep him under wraps in his workouts here, and then they find the right slot for him, put him in it, and turn him loose. Somebody cleans up."

"Jerry Carpenter doesn't need to make money that way," someone else said.

The wise guy just shrugged.

So the suspicious ones toyed with the ringer idea and came up empty. Too many decent people involved. Jerry Carpenter was a great guy, very rich, no need for money. Hank Benson was a top trainer with a thirty-year reputation in the field. Donny Coburn, the jockey who'd ridden King Lear to his surprise win, was the second leading money winner in the East this season, a top pro. The consensus was that the idea of a ringer was a pipe dream. You couldn't get by those three guys with a phony horse. They could have kept King Lear under cover, but it was totally unreasonable for them to involve themselves in a ringer scandal. And so, while the whisper of a scandal went the rounds, nobody took it very seriously in the world of the horse.

Dan Garvey and Julian Quist did not belong to the world of the horse. Garvey in particular, the knot of pain in his gut almost doubling him over, chose not to believe in accidents. The first woman he had ever really loved had been transformed into a bloody piece of hamburger lying in the medical examiner's morgue. Garvey could still hear the sound of her voice, recall the smooth feel of her skin, rejoice in the happy sound of her laughter, almost cry out as he realized that the certainty of her love for him was no longer available. Garvey wasn't accident prone and, by God, Judith at thirty-five had never been accident prone. The only thing that concerned Garvey that first day was punishment: to find the person responsible for Judith's tragic death and drive him into the ground like a fence post.

The beginning point for Garvey had to be Ben Diamond, the stable hand who had tried to rescue Judith from an enraged King Lear—or who had deliberately shot her in the head to cover up a crime she had discovered, or was about to discover.

Ben Diamond probably had a mother who loved him, friends who liked him. To Garvey he was the potential killer of a woman he'd loved. The bullet in Judith's head could have been accidental, but Garvey thought it was much more likely to have been deliberate. He stood at the corner of the short-order counter in Shed Row watching Ben Diamond gulp a cup of coffee he was holding in a shaking hand. Diamond had just been through a severe grilling by Captain Mowery of the State Police—and had been turned loose.

"You know who I am, Diamond?" Garvey asked.

Diamond nodded. "Publicity guy for this whole setup," he said.

"Did you know that Mrs. Cameron and I were going to be married next month?"

"Oh, Jesus!"

"I know you've just given your story to the police," Garvey said. "I'd like to hear it from you myself."

Diamond was not a man of any charm. If he had native wit or humor it had been frightened out of him by what had happened. He was a dark, lanky, well-muscled man with brooding eyes that were bloodshot at the moment. Garvey thought he must actually have been driven to tears by the police grilling. His bony face needed a shave. He was wearing Levis, black cowboy boots, and a pale blue work shirt. His hand shook holding the coffee cup, and even worse when he put down the cup and tried to light a cigarette.

"She was a nice lady," Diamond said, when he got the cigarette going.

Nice! Garvey wanted to hit him, but he kept his voice under control. "You knew her, Diamond?"

"What's 'know her' mean?" Diamond asked. "She was a horse owner who did more than show up in the winner's circle. She was down here at five o'clock every morning while most of them are home in their silk sheets. She was friendly to everyone. She never passed you by without saying 'Good morning,' asking you how things were going in your life, in your barn. I never heard anyone who had anything but good words for her."

"So, this morning you came to work," Garvey prompted.

"Five o'clock," Diamond said. "Every day, I take over from the night watchman then. Guy named Teliski. He's Polish, but not a bad guy, you know? He don't have anything to do with the horses, just guards them. As soon as I come on I feed the horses, grain and hay. After they've et, Ed Smythe—he's the head groom for Mr. Carpenter—and I start to curry and brush and get the animals ready for the day's work. Exercise boys come for our horses about six o'clock."

"This morning," Garvey said sharply. "What happened this morning was around five. To hell with what you do some other day at six!"

Diamond nodded. "Teliski was sitting out in the alley when I got here," he said. "Like always. All quiet, he tells me, and takes off. I go into the tack room. First thing every morning I go into the tack room and make a pot of coffee, electric percolator. Ed Smythe and I drink coffee all morning."

"Good for you," Garvey said, shaken by impatience.

"So I've just got the pot plugged in when I hear this screaming."

Garvey felt his muscles tightening.

"At first I thought it was a horse, you know? They get stung or snagged up on a nail or something, they scream almost like a person. I ran out in the alley and realized it was a person, down the south line of stalls. All the horses had their heads out the top of the stall doors, nervous, snickering. All but one. King Lear! I ran there and—oh, Jesus!"

"Mrs. Cameron was screaming?"

"Not when I got there. The King had drowned her out,

rearing up and coming down on her with his front feet, making that screaming noise—a horse scream."

"But Mrs. Cameron was still alive? What is it, twenty yards from your tack room to the stall? She was screaming when you ran out in the alley, but by the time you reached the stall she wasn't?"

"God Almighty, Mr. Garvey, one kick in the head by that horse and—and her brains could be splattered on the walls!" Diamond reached again for his coffee, but he couldn't raise the cup without spilling.

"I heard you went in the stall," Garvey said.

"I've handled this horse for more than a year, you know?" Diamond said. "I handled him when they raced him in Florida as a two-year-old. I handled him this spring down there. I was one of three men who went to South America with Mr. Carpenter's string. The King was used to me. You could say we were, like, friends. I opened the lower half of the stall door and went in, trying to grab at his halter, calling to him, trying to talk to him. Well, he turned on me, rearing, slashing out at me, eyes wild and crazy."

"You didn't try to help Mrs. Cameron?" Garvey asked.

"My God, Mr. Garvey, you got any idea what it's like to have a crazy horse come at you in a box stall? What is it—like ten feet square? I was lucky to get out of there in one piece and slam the door closed behind me. The bottom half locks automatically, you know? A Yale lock contraption. I didn't know if the lady was dead or alive, but I knew the only chance for her was to get the gun in the tack room and kill the horse." Sweat was beginning to trickle down Diamond's face.

"Is it usual for there to be guns around these stables?" Garvey asked.

"Oh, sure. Every stable has one. Night watchmen have to look out for prowlers. In the daytime you can have a horse hurt, a broken leg, no vet around. You got to be able to put him out of his misery, you know?"

"Go on." Garvey's mouth was a straight, hard slit.

"So I got the gun and I ran back to the stall," Diamond said. "All the time I was yelling for help, but nobody came. I guess I was drowned out by the noise the King was making."

"Nobody else was attracted by that noise?"

"Not right then. It all happened so fast. I got back to the stall and the King was stomping the lady again. I shouted at him and he turned on me. I thought he was going to jump right out the top half of the stall door, trying to get at me. I started—started firing the gun. One of his front feet caught my gun arm, see?" Diamond held out his tanned right arm. He had smeared iodine on a half-circle abrasion. "Ducking out of the way I suppose—I suppose one shot went wild. That must have been the one that caught the lady. But so help me, Mr. Garvey, she was long dead by then. The King went down and I got into the stall and dragged Mrs. Cameron out. There wasn't anything left of her head and face, you know? By then the shots I'd fired brought people running. I had help then, but too late."

"Where was Smythe, the head groom who's supposed to join you at five o'clock?" Garvey asked, fighting nausea.

"Ed was there at the end. Whole thing hadn't lasted more than three minutes."

Three minutes of terror for Judith, trapped in the small area of a box stall with a raging animal. A gentle, kind, sweet person clobbered before she could have realized what was coming.

"How do you account for the horse going berserk?" Garvey asked.

"So help me God, Mr. Garvey, I got no idea," Diamond said. "This was a gentle horse, like a puppy, you know? Always nosing you and whickering for attention. Part of his trouble was he had no fire, no competitive spirit. Just a gentle slob, Ed Smythe called him."

"But he set a track record yesterday."

"And I didn't even have a two-dollar bill on him," Diamond said. "None of us in the stable thought he was out for more than the exercise. He seemed—he seemed a little keyed up when it was over. Took a long time to get him cooled out. But he didn't seem mean or tricky or really overexcited. What turned him on when the lady went into his stall this morning, God only knows."

Garvey stood silent, trying to find a hole in what seemed like a perfectly straight story.

"I'd give anything, Mr. Garvey," Diamond said, "if I could have been quick enough to stop it. She was a nice lady."

The man was like a stuck record, Garvey thought. Nice lady! She had been his lady, the most precious person on earth.

Jerry Carpenter, the owner of King Lear and a score of other quality racehorses, lived a life that a vast majority of Americans simply haven't bothered to imagine. There is always somebody nearby who is richer than you are, by dint of good luck or greater skills or some other special circumstance. Jerry Carpenter would have had to look hard to find anyone as well off as he, let alone better off. He had never had to lift a finger to acquire the luxury that surrounded him. Virgil Carpenter, his great-grandfather, had been one of the nineteenth-century "robber barons" who had first accumulated fortunes in oil, or steel, or railroads, or shipping, like the original Rockefeller, Carnegie, or Mellon. His grandfather had inherited, expanded the Carpenter empire. A great fortune no longer involved one asset, one product. Today one conglomorate owns a multitude of power structures: oil, steel, airlines, television and radio stations, film companies, book publishing firms, hotels, and on and on. No one man any longer runs any one of these mammoth corporations. Interlocking boards of directors, a multitude of experts in scores of different fields, the governments of dozens of countries all over the world, control these kingdoms.

Jerry Carpenter, the fourth generation, had never even been an errand boy in the Carpenter world. He hadn't had to; the money just poured in and he spent it as he chose. If he wanted a house he bought it, or a car, or a half-million-dollar horse, or a fabulous diamond, or whatever on this earth touched his fancy.

He had a reputation for generosity to his friends, to strangers in need, and particularly to medical research. His mother had died of cancer when he was fifteen years old, and the only serious goal in his life was finding a cure for this malignancy. The one thing he'd never bought for himself was a full-time woman. Not that many girls and the mothers of many girls hadn't taken aim at him. He was forty years old the day Judith Cameron came to her violent end. Judith had been a very rich woman who had no need of someone else's money. She couldn't be bought. She and Jerry had adjoining horse farms in Kentucky, had become very good friends, but if Jerry may have had dreams about her, she hadn't responded. Watching her this summer, he became aware, as did many other people, that Judith had finally found the man she wanted, one Daniel Garvey.

"I suppose I was a little jealous," Jerry Carpenter told Quist. "Judith and I were never lovers, you understand, but we loved each other in a sort of brother-and-sister way. At least that's how she felt about me."

The two men were sitting at a corner table in the Stirrup Cup, the elegant restaurant on the grounds of Island Complex. Jerry was a sandy-haired, pleasant-faced, relaxed man without, normally, a serious care in the world. Of the various hobbies he had played with in his life, the thoroughbred racehorse was the one that had stuck. He would have agreed with Willie Jacobs that it was not so much the horses themselves that attracted him but the way of life they represented—"a way of charm and ease and grace and leisure." It is an old-fashioned world that bears very little relation to the real world in which we live, a trip down the rabbit hole with Alice to a magic past.

Neither Jerry Carpenter nor Quist had been interested in lunch. Too much had been going on to upset both their lives. But Quist had finally dragged Jerry away from the press and a small army of friends to a place where they could talk in peace. Jerry was sipping a mint julep, served in a prefrosted glass by a waiter in a scarlet mess jacket. Quist, who foresaw hours ahead before he could relax on the terrace of his Beekman Place apartment and bring Lydia up-to-date, stayed with black iced coffee. He wasn't following Vic Lorch's advice about questions and answers.

"You mentioned Dan Garvey," Quist said, toying with one of his thin black cigars. Nothing tasted quite right this day, not the coffee, not the cigar. "You know him?"

"Of course," Jerry said. "Everybody out here at the Complex knows him. He's done a wonderful job, representing your firm, of course."

"This thing is hell for him," Quist said. "I think he and Judith were close to something permanent."

"After Saratoga was the rumor," Jerry said.

"There are other rumors around—about your horse, Jerry."

"Poor old King Lear," Jerry said. "That 'old' is a term of affection, of course. A three-year-old."

"You bought him from Judith?"

"As a yearling. He's been a joke between us for the last

two years. I bought him from her against her advice. She had a feeling he wasn't going to amount to anything in spite of very good bloodlines. She was pretty smart about those things. 'You can't turn a house pet into a killer dog,' she used to say. A winning racehorse had to have a little of the killer instinct in him. The King didn't have an ounce of it."

Quist's smile was tight. "There seems to be some doubt about that today," he said.

"A clumsy thing to have said. You know what I mean, Julian."

"As a racehorse. But he set a track record yesterday."

"You could have knocked me and my trainer over with the same feather," Jerry said.

"You know people are talking about a ringer?"

"Oh, for God sake, how absurd!"

"How close are you to the daily operation of your stable, Jerry? I have the feeling you aren't a five o'clock in the morning boy."

"I used to be," Jerry said. He lit a cigarette and watched the smoke curl up away from him. "When I'm at Virgil Hills—that's my farm in Kentucky, named after my great-grandfather—I'm an early bird. We breed there, watch the yearlings stretch their legs for the first time. I feel very horsey down there. But at the tracks, starting in Florida, going on to Churchill Downs and Pimlico, and up here to Aqueduct and Belmont and Saratoga in August—and now there's going to be this track here—the social life takes up most of my time. Late nights don't go with early morning workouts. The people who own horses are like a special club, a special fraternity. We live and share a kind of special life."

"And you leave your horses to someone else?"

"I have one of the best trainers in the country, Hank Benson. Ed Smythe, my head groom, has been with Hank for twenty years. I have my own veterinarian, Clem Maguire—a top hand. They've all forgotten more about horses than I've ever learned."

"What about Ben Diamond who shot King Lear this morning?"

"Been with me ten years. He's just a manure shoveler, Julian, but he knows horses. He did the only thing he could do when he saw the King had gone off his rocker. Unfortunately he was too late."

"The people who are talking 'ringer' think the horse who ran that race yesterday in record time wasn't King Lear," Quist said.

"Bullshit!" Jerry said. He was angry. "Hank Benson and Ed Smythe and Ben Diamond have handled that horse every day of his life for the last two years. Ed Smythe and Ben Diamond were in South America with him, just got back a few days ago. You think Hank Benson could have saddled that horse for yesterday's race and not recognized a ringer—even if you could explain how a ringer got into my stable? It's like suggesting a parent wouldn't know his own child from one day to the next."

"So he wasn't a ringer," Quist said. "How do you account for that sudden burst of speed yesterday?"

"The world of the thoroughbred horse is full of surprises," Jerry said. "King Lear was by Bulldozer out of Desert Flower. Those bloodlines almost guarantee speed. That's why I bought him, even when Judith warned me off. He had to run fast, only he didn't until yesterday."

"He developed that killer instinct overnight?"

"Oh God, Julian, who can explain? If Hank Benson had gotten his way, he'd have had me put the King out to grass after his hopeful year—two-year-old. He showed nothing. I insisted he keep him in training." Jerry's laugh was short and bitter. "I wanted him to win just once, even a nothing race, so I'd have the laugh on Judith. So the horse was in shape to run if he could run, would run. He ran three times a week when he was in Buenos Aires. He just ate dust for the whole time he was there. Hank wanted me to send him back to Virgil Hills when they got back here, but I insisted one more try or tries at Aqueduct, Saratoga, and later here. I must have been psychic yesterday and didn't know it. I suggested King Lear be entered in that dog race."

"It costs a lot of money to keep a horse in training who doesn't promise anything," Quist said.

"My dear Julian, I probably sound like a horse's ass to say that money isn't a worry of mine. I could afford this whim if I wanted to." He shook his head. "I never even got a chance to say 'I told you so' to Judith. I guess she had a date with Garvey. I didn't catch up with her after the race. This morning—it was too late, God help us all."

"What did Benson have to say about the race?"

"He was as dumbfounded as I was. Not just that he won. He was running against a second-rate field. But the track record! Would you believe none of us had a nickel on him?"

"Just one of those things," Quist said.

"Yeah."

Quist changed his tack. "What do you think Judith Cameron was doing in King Lear's stall at five o'clock this morning?"

Jerry shrugged his elegant shoulders. "To start with, she is—was—an early bird. Every morning, rain or shine, she'd be out to watch her horses work. And not only her own horses, but like most of us who breed, she always had an interest in the colts and fillies that were bred on the Cameron Farm. King Lear was one of her product. Desert Flower, the dam, is her mare. She'd have an interest in the King after all the hoopla about his setting a track record. She'd also know I was going to give her a hard time. She'd be pleased, of course—not only for me, but selfishly for herself. A track record for the King would up the value of Desert Flower as a brood mare."

"So she drops by your section of Shed Row to have a look at the King. She lets herself into the box stall and the horse attacks her. It was like that, you think?"

"What else can you think?"

"This woman knew horses better than a psychiatrist knows people," Quist said. "Horses were her life. If she saw the King was stirred up, in an excited state, would she let herself into the stall?"

"Might. She might have seen the cause of it."

"Like what?"

Again Jerry's eloquent shoulders moved. "He could have got himself hung up in some way. A horse could try to scratch the side of his head with a hind foot and get that foot caught in the halter. She would go in to free him—him or any horse she saw in that fix."

"So she sets him free and this horse that was more house pet than killer attacks her for the favor?"

"Some kind of an animal could have got in the stall and scared King," Jerry said. "A raccoon. Maybe a snake was forked in with his hay."

"But if the horse was frightened out of his wits by something in his stall, wouldn't Judith have gone for help? The night watchman or Diamond were on duty."

"Unless you knew all the circumstances you can only guess why she acted the way she did," Jerry said. "Whatever those circumstances were, Judith acted in what she thought was the best way."

"Not foolishly?"

"Not Judith. What she did would make sense—if she could tell us."

"Maybe, before we get done with it, she will," Quist said.

He turned, aware that someone was approaching their table. It was Dr. Zabriskie, the track veterinarian, a grey-haired man wearing a blue denim jacket, stained slacks, a white shirt open at the neck. A little lump at one cheek suggested a wad of chewing tobacco. Men who work around stables aren't often smokers.

"Morning, Mr. Quist," the vet said. Then to Jerry Carpenter: "Someone said I'd find you here, Mr. Carpenter. I've just come from the horse hospital where I've been examining King Lear's body."

"Something new?" Jerry asked.

"Plenty," Zabriskie said. His face had a marble-hard look. "That horse had been brutalized, Mr. Carpenter."

"How do you mean—brutalized?"

"There's an area about eight inches square in his stomach that had been hacked at with something sharp—a knife, some kind of pointed iron."

"My God!" Jerry said. "But the shots Diamond fired killed him?"

"No doubt of that," Zabriskie said. "But someone wondered what could have set off a gentle horse so that he'd attack Mrs. Cameron. The wound in his belly isn't all that was done to him. Would you believe it if I told you that somebody stuck a piece of rusty baling wire into that colt's testicles? He must have been in agony you wouldn't believe."

Quist was on his feet. "So I was right!" he said.

"Right?" Jerry asked.

"Judith was murdered," Quist said, his voice harsh. "The horse was used as a cover-up after the fact. Driven to lash out at anything that was there in his stall, which happened to be the dead body of a woman!"

4

Captain Paul Mowery of the State Police was a trim, suntanned man in his mid-forties, blond hair crew cut, grey eyes cold, impersonal, without the remotest spark of humor in them. He didn't like what he was hearing from Julian Quist and Vic Lorch, the Complex's security man.

"If somebody mutilated a horse on the grounds here, it's primarily your job, Mr. Lorch," the trooper captain said.

"It's breaking-and-entering, malicious mischief, vandalism—what have you," Lorch said. "That's police work."

"What I see is murder," Quist said, studying the ash on the end of his thin cigar. The three men were sitting in a corner of the track grandstand. Out on the track horses walked, cantered, galloped under the guidance of exercise boys. Daily routines hadn't been altered by the tragedy that had taken place in the tree-shaded Shed Row area across the way.

Mowery exhibited a kind of painfully controlled patience. "You've heard Ben Diamond's story?" he asked.

"From Vic here," Quist said. "My partner, Dan Garvey,

a close friend of Mrs. Cameron's, went to talk to him but hasn't checked in yet."

"Diamond's story hangs together," Mowery said. "He heard the screaming—both the woman and the horse—ran down the alley, saw what was happening, went back to the tack room to get a gun they kept there, returned, fired wildly. He killed the horse, and one of those wildly fired shots struck Mrs. Cameron, who was almost certainly dead."

"You've heard Dr. Zabriskie's report, Captain?"

Mowery nodded. "Someone, for some reason I can't even guess at yet, deliberately inflicted torturing wounds on the horse. Mrs. Cameron, passing by on the way to her own area of Shed Row, saw the horse in agony, went into the stall to try to help the poor animal, and was killed for her pains."

"She was too horse-wise to do that," Quist said.

"So how else do you account for it?" Mowery asked.

"Right now I think of two possibilities," Quist said. His cigar had gone out and he tossed it away. "One: the lady was killed somewhere else, tossed into the stall, the horse tortured so that it would attack anything and anyone at hand, destroying any evidence of how she really died. Two: there's been talk of a ringer, Captain. The lady could have identified the true King Lear. She raised him. She goes into the stall with a quiet horse to examine him. She is caught there by someone who slugs her—or shoots her. The horse is then tortured and left to destroy the evidence. Maybe Diamond is telling the whole truth. If the lady was slugged, what those iron hooves did to her head afterward would have destroyed any evidence the medical examiner might find of a slugging. One thing is as certain as the rising of the sun, Captain. Mrs. Cameron would never have gone into that stall with a frenzied animal—not alone, not without help."

"She certainly didn't gouge out the horse's gut and drive a wire into its balls," Vic Lorch said. "She certainly didn't bring the attack on herself."

"This ringer theory—is anyone really buying it?" Mowery asked.

"It's been thought of by more than just Mr. Quist," Vic Lorch said. "King Lear couldn't run as fast as he did yesterday, if you go by his record. The animal is so butchered up now it would be hard to prove if there were two horses that looked very much alike. Maybe someone on the Cameron farm in Kentucky who handled King Lear as a yearling—"

"I'm urging you to keep the case open, Captain," Quist said.

Mowery stood up. "I can only report facts, not theories, to my superiors."

"You can tie up loose ends. You can put a stop to rumors," Quist said.

"How?"

"If the horse who ran at Aqueduct yesterday was a ringer, how do you account for the fact that neither Hank Benson, the trainer; Ed Smythe, the groom; Ben Diamond, the stable hand; Donny Coburn, the jockey who rode him—none of them spotted the substitution of another horse? They'd all handled King Lear for almost two years."

"Because he wasn't a ringer," Mowery said. "The horse just came to life on that particular day."

"But if they all knew he was a ringer, they all cleaned up on his winning," Quist said. "There must be a way to trace down, Captain, who cleaned up substantially on bets. What about bank accounts? What about any splurge spending last night, after the race? Do any of those four men have wives, or women? Maybe the spending won't take place for a while because of what's happened. The men and their women can be watched, can't they?"

Mowery shook his head, stubbornly. "The woman was kicked to death by a crazy horse. Diamond tried to save her and in the process fired a wild shot into her head. Your own argument doesn't hold water, Quist. Hank Benson has a fine reputation, thirty years on the local tracks; Ed Smythe, too. Coburn is one of the top jockeys. Only Ben Diamond is a nobody. According to you they all handled the horse. So if there was a ringer scheme, they all had to be in on it. That I just can't buy. They can't all have turned crooked at the same time. One of them, maybe. But then wouldn't one of the others have spotted it? I urge you, Mr. Quist, don't stir up a hornet's nest. It won't be good for the Complex. You'll smear a lot of innocent people. Mrs. Cameron was killed by a frenzied horse."

"And who tortured the horse, and why?" Quist asked.

"We'll keep at that. And Lorch here will keep at that," Mowery said.

"I hope I don't grow old waiting for you to come up with an answer," Quist said. The slowness of police routine had a way of driving him up the wall.

As Willie "Slick" Jacobs had said, he knew everyone worth knowing in the world of the horse. Years around the various tracks had brought him into frequent contact with Hank Benson, Jerry Carpenter's trainer.

"Carpenter's lucky to get Hank," Willie told Quist as they drove across the Island to Aqueduct where the racing was that afternoon. "He's saddled horses for some of the biggest owners in the business. He's handling two other stables beside Carpenter's at the moment—Paul Quigley's string and the French count, Remy de Beauville."

"Doesn't that make for a conflict of interests?" Quist

asked, his eyes on the road. The afternoon's racing was already well underway at Aqueduct and the approach roads were clear.

"Common practice," Willie said. "But if a trainer has two horses going, same or different owners, they have to run as an entry. Same odds on both horses. In other words, you bet on the entry. No money advantage for the trainer to favor one horse over the other. Hank Benson has had two Derby winners over the years, two Preaknesses, and you'd need a computer to keep track of the number of stake races he's taken. This guy doesn't have to fix races, Julian, or sneak in ringers. He's got it made. He can write his own ticket with someone like Jerry Carpenter. He's probably into Jerry for something like telephone numbers."

They were between races at Aqueduct as Quist and Willie made their way toward the saddling enclosure where Willie was sure they would find Benson. A happy crowd moved around the circular space where horses were getting their last touches, jockeys in their bright colors waiting to be put up on their mounts.

"If we'd got here soon enough I'd have a few bucks on Damask Queen. Short odds but a sure thing. Best filly of this year's crop," Willie said. "There's Benson, next to the last enclosure down the line. Carpenter has a filly named Bessie Watty who might give the Queen her only trouble."

Benson was a grey man: grey hair, grey tropical worsted suit, grey shirt, pale blue tie the color of his eyes. He was standing at the head of a chestnut filly who seemed unconcerned by the crowd or by an awareness that her moment was just ahead. Benson was talking to a jockey in the pink-and-grey colors of the Carpenter stables. Quist and Willie stopped a few yards away, listening.

"That's Donny Coburn who rode King Lear yesterday," Willie said, indicating the jockey. "One of the very best."

"Damask Queen will settle in about fourth, depending on the pace," Benson was telling his rider. "She won't make her move till halfway down the backstretch. Stick with her, and when she takes off, you take off." He reached up and stroked the filly's neck. "Then it will just be a case of who can run faster."

"You think Bessie can do it?" Coburn asked.

"She needs a little luck," Benson said. "Let the Queen take a false step, change leads at the wrong time on the turn, and Bessie could breeze. Just let her go, Donny. She'll give you all she's got without you going to the whip."

"I got you, Mr. Benson," the jockey said.

"Hi, Hank," Willie said. "This is Julian Quist, who handles all the promotion over at the Complex."

"I know," Benson said. He gave Quist's pink linen suit a disapproving look.

"All hell's broken loose over at the Complex," Willie said. "Talk about murder. Talk about a ringer going for King Lear yesterday."

"Pure crap," Benson said. "About the ringer, I mean."

"I understand you saddled King Lear for yesterday's race, Benson," Quist said.

"That's track language, Mr. Quist," Benson said. "All trainers 'saddle' their horses. That doesn't mean they actually tighten the saddle girths, check the stirrup lengths, put the jockey up. As a matter of fact, I wasn't even in the enclosure when King Lear was readied yesterday. Ed Smythe, my groom, did the actual saddling. I was up in the clubhouse talking to Paul Quigley, one of my owners."

"So you didn't actually see the horse that was saddled?"

"I didn't see him here in the enclosure, but I saw him run. Damn near died of a heart attack."

Donny Coburn, the jockey, giggled. He was a thirty-year-old child. "Ed Smythe told me I should take a flashlight with me. We might be late getting back in. I damn near didn't get back at all. Lear took off so fast he almost left me behind him in the starting gate."

"But you rode him. You know it was King Lear?" Quist asked.

"Tell you the truth, I never saw him before," the jockey said.

"Donny is a contract rider for Jerry Carpenter," Benson explained. "That means we have first call on his services. But we never used him except for the best horses in the big races. Like today. But yesterday—?" Benson shrugged. "We were running King Lear, just to please Jerry. He insisted that someday the King would win one and he'd have the laugh on Mrs. Cameron—poor lady. An apprentice rider, Billy Coffin, was supposed to ride the King, but in the race before he got his hand jammed in the starting gate. I had nobody to put up on the King. Donny was supposed to ride the next race so he was here. I asked him to ride the King—as a favor to Jerry."

"I owe Jerry a lot," Coburn said. "Smythe told me this was going to be like an exercise gallop. No problems except the horse wouldn't run."

"And you'd never seen the King before?" Quist asked.

"Maybe. Around the stable. But I never paid him any attention. He wasn't a horse I was going to handle."

"So you wouldn't know if the horse you rode yesterday was a ringer or not?"

Coburn laughed. "Would you believe that down the backstretch I asked myself if Ed had made a mistake and given me the wrong horse. He took off like a rocket and never stopped running!"

"So Coburn didn't know him and you didn't see him," Quist said to Benson.

"You're way off base, Mr. Quist. I saw him run. I saw him

when we got him back to the Complex later in the afternoon."

"Switched on the way over here, switched on the way back," Quist suggested.

Benson was controlling anger. "By Martians? Oh, come on, Mr. Quist. Ed Smythe and Ben Diamond trucked the King over here from the Complex—in our truck. They were with him the whole time he was here, and they trucked him back to the Complex after the race—in our truck. No possible way for a switch."

"Unless they were both in on it," Quist said.

A bugle sounded in the distance.

"Parade to the post," Benson said. "Up you go, Donny. Sorry, no more time for this nonsense of yours, Mr. Quist."

"Is Smythe here somewhere?" Quist asked.

"He took the day off," Benson said. "He was pretty shook up by what happened to Mrs. Cameron."

"And to the horse?"

Benson had been about to give Coburn a lift up onto the filly, but he hesitated. "What are you talking about?"

"You haven't heard that someone gouged out the horse's gut with some kind of a knife, that someone rammed a piece of baling wire into his testicles?"

"Jesus Christ!" Benson said. He looked stunned.

"We gotta get going, Hank," the jockey said.

Like a man in a trance, Benson mounted Coburn and watched Bessie Watty move out into the parade to the post. He watched until the horses with their riders in bright colored silks disappeared into the tunnel that led to the track. Then he turned to Quist. "I don't believe it," he said.

"It's an ugly fact, Hank," Willie Jacobs said.

It was possible, Willie Jacobs thought, that a ringer could have been "rung in" on Hank Benson. The trainer, Willie reported to Quist, was handling a couple of dozen active horses for Carpenter, Paul Quigley and the French Count Remy de Beauville. By "active" Willie meant horses that were actually racing at the current meet, which was at Aqueduct.

"He wrote off King Lear months ago," Willie said, "but he kept him active to please Jerry Carpenter. That doesn't mean that he looked him over every day personally. He'd given up on him. He'd get a stable report from Ed Smythe every day. As long as the exercise boys didn't report that King Lear showed some sign of soreness in his workouts, as long as he hadn't developed a splint or any minor injury, there'd be no need to check on him personally. Ed Smythe was capable of caring for the King, scheduling his workouts. Benson wasn't really interested in him anymore."

"But Benson saw him win that race," Quist said. They were driving back across the Island to the Complex.

"He was in the clubhouse, which isn't exactly on the rail," Willie said. "He sees a bay colt with black mane and tail, black leg markings, come out in the parade to the post. He sees the Carpenter colors, pink and grey. It's not a close-up picture, you understand? He expects to see King Lear with Donny Coburn up, so that's what he sees."

"And he sees speed he didn't think the horse had in him," Quist said. "No doubts or questions then?"

"Horses are full of surprises," Willie said. "It's in the charts. You wouldn't remember Elkridge, the old steeple-chaser. The first race he ran for his owner he was last, by a hundred lengths. That's not an exaggeration. Like I say, you'll find it in the charts. The next time out Elkridge finished last, but this time only fifty lengths behind. That is what we call a dog-meat horse. Like King Lear. Elkridge's owner kept going with him because he was like a pet, and he was the first horse that owner ever owned. You could put a lump of sugar between your lips and Elkridge would take it from you, gentle as can be. But in the end, after a number of years, old Elkridge had set a record for the most money ever won by a steeplechaser. So when Benson sees King Lear flying to a new track record, he just thinks its one of those things, one of those miracles that make the world of the horse so unpredictable and so exciting."

"But he isn't interested enough to go check on his winner?"

"He's got plenty of time. He's got other horses running that day. He'll look King Lear over when he's back at the Complex. Maybe the next day. Ed Smythe reports the horse has come out of the race sound. He'll believe in real miracles when he sees the horse run the next time—which, of course, he never will."

"So you really think Benson could have been had?"

Willie nodded. "But not Ed Smythe. He tightened the saddle girths on King Lear—if it was King Lear—and he put Donny Coburn up. He fed that horse a lump of sugar or a carrot every day for two years. No way in the world Ed Smythe could have been fooled."

"So there is no ringer. Or Ed Smythe is the villain of the piece," Quist said.

"That's the way the script reads," Willie said. "So we'll ask him."

Among the vast store of information about the world of the horse that Willie Jacobs kept stored in his head just happened to be the location of the cottage Ed Smythe rented about a mile from Shed Row at the Complex.

"I always know where people I might want to talk to live," Willie said.

"What made you think you might want to talk to Ed Smythe someday?" Quist asked.

"He handles horses that run for money," Willie said. He

gave Quist a sly smile. "It's a regret to me that a sport of such elegance and grace should be so closely related to the cash register. I regret, equally, that I must eat, and clothe myself, and buy a little booze, and that my only source of revenue is that same cash register. To make that work you have to know a little more than the average schmucks who crowd up to the mutuel windows to lose their money. So it is important to me to be on a friendly footing with the people who prepare the horses to do their running. You get your edge on that cash register by listening."

"To what?"

"Information the touts don't get. You make friends with an Ed Smythe and a couple of dozen others like him, and they'll tell you when a horse is ready and when it isn't. That's enough of an edge for me."

"So you trust Ed Smythe?"

"About horses," Willie said.

"But he didn't tell you King Lear was ready?"

"No, the sonofabitch didn't. I could have made myself a summer vacation on that one."

"But your opinion of him as a man, Willie?"

They were tooling along the thruway, the late afternoon sun turning the ocean, to their right, gold and green. Quist, at the wheel, had produced a pair of black sunglasses to shield his eyes from the glare.

"A man of excesses," Willie said. "Ed is big—six feet five, maybe, three hundred pounds. Big eater, like three steaks, eggs, potatoes, toast for breakfast. Loud voice that shatters windowpanes except when he's talking to a horse, and then he's as soft and silky as a lady in love. Loves to gamble at cards, which has kept him broke half his life. Even the kids around Shed Row will take him at five-card stud or blackjack. He likes women, different women, a lot of women—which also eats away at his paycheck. But he is so good with young horses that I guess Jerry Carpenter has bailed him out more times than you could count. He's been in trouble with loan sharks who don't play for fun, you know what I mean? A colorful guy, expert at his trade, and a prime candidate for Gamblers Anonymous."

"A guy who can be driven that far could go for a ringer scheme or a fix," Quist said.

Willie shook his head, slowly. "You'd have to know Ed well before you'd make that kind of a judgment on him," he said. "He loves food, he loves women, he loves cards, but he really *loves* horses. I don't think he would foul up on a horse he was handling for anything on earth. Hank Benson is always lecturing Ed about his life style, but he puts up with it because he knows the horses Ed handles will get TLC."

"TLC?"

"Tender, loving care," Willie said. "Next right, Julian."

A narrow side road led to the cottage where Ed Smythe lived. It was a grey, shingle cottage facing the ocean. It must once have been a valuable property before the new thruway cut almost through the backyard of the place.

"It was a steal when Jerry Carpenter bought it a couple of years ago," Willie said, as they pulled up by the front door. "He thought Hank Benson would like it—near the new track and all. But Hank has lived in hotel rooms and motel rooms all his life. Didn't want to bother to take care of it. Ed jumped at the chance to use it. Great place to bring his women."

"No car around," Quist said. He had cut off the motor of his Mercedes. He could hear the waves breaking on the beach a hundred yards away. "Maybe he went somewhere else to get over being shocked."

Willie hopped out of the car and went to the front door. He beat on it with the brass knocker. "Ed! You in there?"

Evidently there was no answer. Quist watched Willie go

around to a side window and, shielding his eyes, peer inside. Then Willie stepped back and seemed to freeze where he stood. He turned and beckoned urgently to Quist.

Quist got out of the car and crossed the sun-browned lawn to where the little man stood.

"Listen!" Willie said. He pointed to the closed door of the garage at the rear of the cottage. Quist heard it. There was a car in the garage with the motor running.

Willie ran to the garage door and lifted it up. He stepped back, choking.

"Oh my God!" Willie cried out.

The huge body of Ed Smythe lay on the floor behind the car. A piece of rubber tubing led from the car's exhaust pipe into a plastic bag over Smythe's head.

Willie ducked in past the man on the floor and turned off the car motor.

"Help me drag him out," he said.

Quist stood very still. "No use, Willie," he said. "It's been too late for quite a while. This is one for the cops."

A crooked horse race, the murder of a lovely lady, and the suicide of a wise man who knew all the angles was enough to stand the world of the horse on its collective ears. The track stewards at Aqueduct, the governing body of the New York Racing Association, and the thousands of people who read the *Daily Racing Form* were concerned about the dead horse and his suicidal groom. Had there been a ringer scandal? Had Ed Smythe, heretofore trusted, been a party to it and stuck his head in a plastic bag where all he could breath was carbon monoxide? Most of these people passed by the death of Judith Cameron. A regrettable accident at the least, a possible murder at the juicy best. To them the manipulation of a dead horse by a dead handler was the key story.

To Quist the murder of Judith Cameron was all that

concerned him. Let the world of the horse take care of its own crooked maneuverings. Murder was murder in any world, and the murder of a friend of Quist's and the bride-to-be of Garvey's wasn't just an interesting puzzle. Garvey would never draw a breath without pain until he had the killer, so to speak, nailed to the barn door. Quist was aiming at the same target.

Captain Mowery of the State Police had the case wrapped up in his own mind. He no longer resisted the idea that Judith Cameron had been murdered, but he was satisfied that the murderer lay dead in a garage with a hose from a car exhaust in his mouth.

"It's a confession," Mowery said to Quist.

It was after dark then, the yard around the little shingle cottage crowded with police cars and the ambulance from the morgue, searchlights from the tops of cars lighting the grim scene. Mowery had developed a satisfactory story that would close the case.

"The horse was a ringer," Mowery said.

"Hank Benson satisfy you on that?"

Mowery didn't like the question. "Officially? A flat, out-and-out statement? No. The animal's body is pretty badly mutilated. Gunshots blew its head apart. Thoroughbreds have a lip tattoo, an identifying mark inside the upper lip. Damage to the horse's head obliterated that mark. That tattoo should have answered the question permanently."

"But don't they check those identifying tattoos before or after a race?" Quist asked.

Mowery shrugged. "Maybe there's some kind of an artist with a tattoo needle somewhere who could change things so they'd pass a casual look by a track official. Point is we can't tell now.

"Benson says King Lear had a little patch of white hair on his stomach about the size of a half-dollar. Some minor injury he suffered as a yearling. But that patch of white hair was eliminated by the knife wounds someone inflicted. You have to think that someone tried to make identification impossible. So Benson says the dead horse could have been a ringer, but also a ringer in the nonprofessional sense of the word. If he was a ringer he was almost an identical twin of King Lear's. Same weight, same height, same conformation. The best Benson will say is that the animal was 'probably' a ringer. If he was, Ed Smythe knew. I think we can depend on that. He caught the lady giving the horse a too careful once-over. He went down to the tack room, got the gun he kept there, and shot the lady. Then he brutalized the horse and left it to destroy the evidence."

"Hold everything!" Quist said. "Where was Ben Diamond when all this was going on, or Teliski the night watchman?"

"I haven't been able to locate Diamond since this morning."

"You let him go."

"I know. I still think he was telling the truth."

"The gun was apparently fully loaded when he is supposed to have done what he says he did. If Smythe used it—"

"Maybe he reloaded it before he put it back."

"And all the time the horse and the woman were screaming down the alley?"

"Maybe not," Mowery said. "Maybe Smythe shot the woman, replaced the gun, and then went back to brutalize the horse."

"And Teliski?"

"Teliski admits he was missing from his post for about ten minutes before five o'clock. Night watchman in the stables of the Count de Beauville, which is just down the line, was taken sick. He asked Teliski to take a look at his horses. Smythe, due at five, came a few minutes early, found the woman in the stall with the horse, found Teliski missing, no one around. He acted. Then Diamond arrives, makes his coffee, hears the screaming, and goes down the line to find the horse stomping the woman. He goes and gets the gun and does what he says he did."

"And then takes a powder when you release him."

"It was a pretty disturbing experience for him," Mowery said. "He'll turn up when he hears about this." He gestured toward the men who were carrying the giant body of Ed Smythe toward the morgue ambulance.

"Diamond says Teliski was at his post when he arrived at five o'clock," Quist said.

"We're talking about a stretch of time a little before five," Mowery said. "Ten minutes, fifteen minutes. Teliski was checking for his friend. Smythe arrives, finds the woman in with the horse, does his thing. When Diamond arrives, Teliski is back. Smythe is down the alley in Shed Row, brutalizing the horse. The screaming starts. Smythe slips away."

"And then he comes over here and kills himself," Quist said. "The car motor was running when Willie Jacobs and I found him, going on six o'clock. He took quite a while to decide what to do. The car still has half a tank of gas in it. He couldn't have decided to kill himself until late in the afternoon. How did he spend the day?"

"We questioned him early in the morning, along with Diamond," Mowery said. "No reason to hold him—at that time." He drew a deep breath. "So you were right, Mr. Quist. It was murder, and the case is closed."

"Diamond said he fired four shots, didn't he? Where is the fourth bullet if Smythe fired the one that killed Mrs. Cameron?"

"Diamond didn't say he fired four shots," Mowery said. "He didn't remember how many shots he fired—just till the horse dropped. We found four bullets and assumed he fired four times. Two unfired shells in the gun. But now I think there's no doubt Smythe shot the woman and Diamond actually only fired three shots at the horse."

"So there should have been three unfired shells in the gun if Smythe reloaded it. It's a six-shooter."

"So Smythe didn't take time to reload it," Mowery said. "Or if he did, we'll find that there's a fourth bullet in the straw, or maybe it went out a window and is somewhere outside on the grounds."

"Or Diamond is lying and is responsible for the whole thing," Quist said.

"They why would Smythe kill himself?"

"That could be the sixty-four-thousand-dollar question, Captain," Quist said.

It was after midnight when Quist let himself into his duplex apartment on Beekman Place. The last forty-five minutes, driving in from the Island, he had felt an urgent need to be there. It had been an ugly day, a day of violence and bloodshed, the death of a lady he had admired and liked and who mattered so very much to Dan Garvey, the butchering of a thoroughbred animal, and finally the suicide of a man who had been trusted all his life in his own special world.

It seemed to Quist that every muscle in his body ached. He needed to be free of the tensions of the outside world, needed the peace and security and delight of being with Lydia.

Lydia Morton had come into Quist's life a few years back. She was a dark-haired, very lovely girl with the elegant figure of a fashion model, a wry sense of humor, and the gift of calm efficiency in crisis. Dealing with Quist's high-powered clients was, in a way, a state of permanent crisis.

It was not surprising that two unusually attractive people with complementing talents should have come together in a love affair. It would have been surprising had they not. What did surprise Quist's staff and his friends was that the relationship became locked into an unshakeable permanence. Quist, before Lydia, had not been unlike Dan Garvey in his womanizing. Women went for him and he for them. One day, like turning on a light switch, his whole life style changed. There was Lydia and no one else. She shared his living quarters with him, shared his dreams, shared his disappointments and his problems. She became a partner in his business and a partner in his life. Some people asked why they hadn't married. It was quite simple, and they both felt the same way about it. What they had was so perfect neither of them chose to risk the slightest change.

She was waiting just inside the apartment door when he let himself in. She was wearing a wine-red housecoat, her dark hair hanging long to her shoulders. George, the night doorman, had called her when he saw Quist crossing to the elevator.

"The boss is on his way up."

They didn't speak at first. Quist just took her in his arms and held her very close. Then he took her by the shoulders and held her gently away from him, looking down at her.

"Thanks for being here," he said. "It's been one hell of a day."

"Dan?" she asked.

"Lost him somewhere. He's out to get someone."

"Poor Dan. Drink?"

"Oh, brother! Would you?"

They sat on the terrace overlooking the East River. The running lights of a barge moved slowly downstream. Quist, his legs stretched out in a deck chair, sipped the double Jack

Daniels on the rocks with a splash of water she'd brought him. She didn't have to ask what he wanted.

Gradually, piece by piece, he told her about his day; about his early certainty that Judith Cameron's death was not a hideous accident. When he had finished and she had brought him his second drink, she asked a question. He had done all the talking up to then.

"You don't buy Captain Mowery's solution?"

"It could be the way he thinks it was," he said, swirling the whiskey over the ice cubes in his glass. "In any case it's a quick answer that may satisfy a lot of people."

"But not you?"

"If you'd heard Willie Jacobs about Smythe, you might share my doubts. He loved food, Willie said. He loved women, he loved cards, but he really *loved* horses. A loud voice that shatters windowpanes, but when he talks to a horse it's as soft and silky as a lady in love. Would such a man gouge out a horse's gut and ram a piece of baling wire into his parts?"

"To cover up a murder?"

"Maybe. But that man, with that love of horses—wouldn't he have tried some other way first?"

"How hot was the heat?" Lydia asked.

The telephone just inside the French doors to the terrace rang. It was nearly one thirty in the morning.

"It could be Dan," Quist said, as Lydia went to answer it.

It wasn't Garvey. It was George, the night man in the lobby.

"There's a lady down here who says she must see Mr. Quist, Miss Morton."

"Who is she, George?"

"She says her name is Rosemary Wilson. She says Mr. Quist doesn't know her, but that it's very important."

Quist came to the phone when Lydia reported.

"Put the lady on, George," he said.

"Mr. Quist?" It was a husky, low voice, unsteady.

"Yes. What can I do for you, Miss Wilson?"

"I have to talk to you, Mr. Quist. You see, I'm sure I know who murdered Mrs. Cameron."

PART TWO

1

It would be inaccurate to say that Rosemary Wilson was unexpected, because in fact Quist and Lydia had no basis on which to expect anything. It took only about three minutes for her to arrive at the front door after her startling announcement on the house phone.

"Some kind of a nut," Quist guessed.

He and Lydia had moved from the terrace to the living room with its modern furniture, the far-out modern paintings on the wall, the little service bar in the corner, the carefully designed, almost theatrical lighting that divided the room into areas of brightness and shadow. Quist waited at the front door and opened it the instant the door buzzer sounded.

Rosemary Wilson faced him, with George, the night man, standing just behind her.

"Okay, Mr. Quist?" George asked.

"Thanks, George," Quist said. "Come in, Miss Wilson."

Miss Wilson was short, Twiggy-thin, looking almost like a young boy in her blue jeans and Tattersall vest that covered a man's white shirt, open at the throat. Her red hair was boyish cut. Her eyes were a very bright blue, filled at the moment with doubt and perhaps a little fear. She was tanned from much exposure to sunshine, but the tan didn't hide a bridge of freckles across her straight little nose. Quist remembered that he'd always been a sucker for freckles. His first girl, when he was eight, had sported freckles.

The girl took a hesitant step into the room, looking around as though she'd never seen a place quite like this before.

"This is Miss Morton," Quist said.

"Hi," Lydia said. "Come in and sit down, won't you, Miss Wilson."

The girl looked at one of the chromium-trimmed armchairs as though it might be a trap. She took a chance, slipping the strap of her large leather bag off her shoulder and putting it down on the floor beside her. She looked a little surprised. The chair was comfortable.

Quist held a lighter to one of his thin, black cigars. "What you had to say on the phone—?"

"I'm sure I know," the girl said.

"Then let me ask you a question before we go into it," Quist said. "Why me? Why aren't you talking to the police?"

"Because they've made up their minds," Rosemary Wilson said. She looked from Quist to Lydia and back again. "You see, Ed Smythe was my father."

Quist showed no surprise. "Is it Mrs. Wilson, then?"

The girl shook her head. "Wilson was my mother's name," she said. "Ed never married anyone."

Neither Quist nor Lydia commented. The girl twisted nervously in the chrome-trimmed chair. "Willie Jacobs said you were the one to talk to, Mr. Quist."

"You know Willie, then?"

"All my life."

"Which can't be more than twenty years," Quist said.

"My next birthday, which is in September. I wanted Willie to call you, to vouch for me. But when I decided to come I couldn't find him."

"All right, Rosemary, let's start at the beginning—wherever that is," Quist said. "And let's cut the formalities. I'm Julian. Miss Morton is Lydia."

"Thank you—Julian," Rosemary said. She smiled, shyly, at Lydia.

"Would you like some coffee?" Lydia asked her.

The blue eyes drifted toward the bar. "If—if you have a drink of some sort. I feel as if I were about to cave in."

"Any sort. Name your poison," Quist said.

"If you had just a thimbleful of brandy—"

Lydia went to the bar and brought back a drink for the girl. She found herself feeling protective. She guessed that Quist was having much the same reaction.

Rosemary sipped her drink. "That's so very good."

"Take your time," Quist said.

The girl put her half-finished drink down on the table beside her chair. "My mother was—was a professional," she said. "A prostitute. Poor old Ed liked professional women. He had no feeling of obligation to them—afterwards. But he was always kind, and thoughtful, and full of laughter. Any professional gal he'd spent time with could go to him for help, and he'd give it."

"He knew about you?" Quist asked.

"Of course! My mother died when I was five years old. There was a fire in a hotel where she was—was working. She didn't get away. Ed took charge of my life then. I was placed in a foster home, but he'd come to see me every day when he was here. Of course in the winter he'd take off for Florida, for Hialeah, Churchill Downs, Pimlico. This last winter he went to South America for two months. He'd always send me postcards. I always knew where he was in case I needed him. I loved him, Julian. I loved him very much."

"And so, naturally, you don't believe he killed Mrs. Cameron."

"I *know* he didn't!"

"How do you know so certainly?"

"Because Ed was Ed," she said, and reached for her drink to take another sip.

"The police aren't likely to listen to that as a reason," Quist said. "They'll say some kind of special pressure drove him to it. For example, King Lear wasn't King Lear."

"I don't think he was," Rosemary said.

Quist glanced at Lydia. "Why?" he asked.

"Since I was ten years old," Rosemary said, "I've spent most of the summers with Ed, at Belmont, and Aqueduct, and Saratoga. He taught me about horses, he loved them so much. I began to walk horses, and exercise some of them. I—I'm very good with horses, thanks to Ed. There are a lot of girls around the tracks these days, doing that kind of thing. There are even a few girl jockeys."

"I know."

"But I had the best teacher of all of them. All the happiness I've ever had came from learning from Ed, from spending my summers with him at the tracks. I could hire out to any number of stables now, have been offered jobs, but I stayed with Ed—because he was Ed."

"We're getting away from the point, Rosemary," Quist said quietly. "You say you think the King Lear who won that stake race day before yesterday was a ringer?"

Rosemary leaned forward in her chair. "Please, Julian, whatever I tell you is between us—you and me and Lydia—until we can prove something, flat out. What I think could be worse than murder, and if it's just something I've dreamed up—"

"Willie Jacobs must have made you believe you could trust us," Quist said.

Rosemary leaned back in her chair, and for a moment her eyelids fluttered, closed. "I think the whole trouble started this past winter in South America. I saw them off, Ed and Ben Diamond and the horses. Ed was feeling great, riding high, on top of the wave. It was to be a new experience." She smiled a tight little smile. "New women."

"Women in every port, I take it."

"Next to horses, the greatest sport on earth to Ed was women. The day they took off I said a special goodbye to King Lear. He was one of the horses I'd been allowed to work with, probably because Ed thought he wasn't worth anything. Couldn't run a lick. But he was a sweet animal, and Jerry Carpenter insisted he have a chance in South America. There's no question the horse I said goodbye to was King Lear. I couldn't mistake him any more than you could mistake your own pet dog." She hesitated. "But the horse that came back two months later—? I was shut away from him, not allowed to walk him or exercise him. Ed said I was ready for something better than King Lear, and he gave me a really good filly to work with—Clothilda. I was delighted."

"And you had nothing more to do with King Lear?"

"Oh, I'd stop by his stall to talk to him. He seemed changed, a little standoffish. When you fly horses any distance they react in all kinds of different ways. Like jet lag in people. I figured Lear would get to be his old self after a while."

"But he didn't?"

"No. But I was too busy with my new horse to pay much attention. Then I saw him run, day before yesterday—new track record for a mile and a furlong. I wondered then. King Lear could never run like that."

"But he looked like King Lear? This standoffish colt that came back from South America looked like King Lear?"

"An exact twin," Rosemary said. "But let me tell you something, Julian. King Lear was sired by the great Bulldozer. I've seen half a dozen of Bulldozer's sons out of different dams, and they look so much alike you'd find yourself asking, 'Is that my horse or your horse?' "

"So Ed could have brought a different colt back from South America? He'd have to know it was a different colt, wouldn't he? He and Ben Diamond would have to know, wouldn't they?"

Rosemary sat very still, staring at the remains of the brandy in her glass. "King Lear seemed changed when he got back from South America. But that was nothing compared to the change in Ed. A different man, an anxious man, I might even say a frightened man."

"Frightened of what?"

"Of his own shadow, it seemed like," Rosemary said.

"Let's try beginning there," Quist said.

Rosemary moistened her lips. "That's what I came to talk to you about," she said.

You couldn't push her. She has to tell it her own way, Quist thought. Her voice was unsteady as she went on.

"Ed wasn't Ed when he came back with the horses from South America," she said. "He hardly noticed me when I went to meet him, which hurt a little. He had a lot on his mind, I knew. There were horses to be stabled at the Complex and others at Aqueduct. There were money accountings to make to Jerry Carpenter on the South American trip. But he—he acted almost as though he wanted to avoid me. Three nights ago I decided to go see him at his cottage to find out, if I could, what was wrong between us. Ed had faults, you understand: women, gambling, a monstrous eater. But one thing he didn't do was hit the sauce."

"No liquor?" Quist asked.

"Oh, he might have a beer or two at the end of a big day, a glass of wine with a meal. Hard liquor, never. But three nights ago when I went to see him at his cottage he was stoned, out cold. From the empty bottles and the smell of the room where I found him passed out on a bed, I knew he had really poured it on. I tried to rouse him, but I couldn't at first. I made him some hot black coffee and tried to force him to drink it. He came to a little, but it was a while before he seemed to recognize me. At first I think he thought I was some woman he'd brought there with him."

"Tough for you, Rosemary," Lydia said.

"I was scared at first. I thought he'd really done himself some harm. I thought of calling a doctor. But, suddenly, he knew me. He put his big arms around me and he was actually crying. 'Rosie! Rosie!' he said. 'My darling little Rosie!' He drank some of the coffee, and then he sat looking at me out of his swollen eyes, shaking his head from side to side. 'I sold out, Rosie,' he said. 'Something I never thought I'd do. Oh, God, I sold out!' And then he passed out again."

"He didn't tell you what he meant?"

"Not then," Rosemary said. "I didn't try to rouse him again. I thought he was talking crazy, you see? I sat there all night, keeping him covered with a light blanket. It's cool down there at the beach. It was long after daylight when he came to again. He seemed surprised to see me. He asked me what I was doing there, when I'd come. I told him the night before. He sat bolt upright in bed, like a great mountain. 'What did I tell you?' he wanted to know. 'Nothing, really,' I told him. 'Some crazy talk about selling out.' 'Oh my God,' he said, and covered his face with his hands. After a long time he looked at me again. 'I've often heard people say that every man has his price,' he said. 'I didn't believe it. I knew I didn't. But God help me, Rosie, I did.'

"I tried to make light of it. I laughed at him. 'So what was your price?' I asked him, wondering what he could have sold out. 'Part of a forty-seven-million-dollar deal,' he said. I laughed again. 'You got forty-seven million dollars?' I said. 'So let's take a trip to the moon! What on earth are you talking about?' 'A piece of forty-seven million dollars,' he said. 'A big enough piece so I'd never have to worry again, never have to go to the loan sharks again, never have to do without anything I wanted again.' I still thought he was kidding. Forty-seven million dollars! 'So what did you sell that was worth a piece of forty-seven million dollars?' I asked him.

"He took me by the shoulders and shook me like a rag doll. 'Don't you ever ask me that, Rosie,' he shouted. 'Don't you ever repeat a word of what I've said to you here if you want to go on living.' I—I thought he was threatening me for a moment, and that really scared me. And then he said, 'They'll kill you if they think I've told you anything.' 'Who are they?' I asked him. He let go of me and began to cry again, great, huge sobs. 'Get out of here, Rosie,' he said. 'Go away from here! Forget that I ever meant anything to you. Forget anything I've said to you. Your life may depend on it!' He got up, grabbed me, and literally threw me out of the house. That's the last time I saw him, Julian."

Done with the telling, the girl began to cry softly, shaken by the memory.

"A phony horse, replacing King Lear, couldn't have meant forty-seven million dollars to anyone, could he?" Lydia asked.

"Of course not," Quist said. "A few thousand may have been made on him, maybe a few tens of thousands. You could hear the screams all over the country if any huge sums had been bet on him. Forty-seven million is a telephone number, love."

Rosemary raised her tear-stained face. "I had to believe at the time it was all some kind of drunken exaggeration," she said. "Like hearing someone say they'd have made a billion dollars on some deal if they'd been smart enough."

"Forty-seven million is a very exact number," Quist said. "Not forty million, or fifty million, but exactly forty-seven million."

"He didn't mention King Lear? He didn't mention any other kind of deal?" Lydia asked.

"Only that, 'they,' whoever 'they' are, would kill me if they thought he had told me. But I know, Julian, that nothing on earth could have forced Ed to kill Mrs. Cameron or torture any horse. 'They' must have done it!"

"You didn't ask him about King Lear?" Lydia asked.

"You forget the King hadn't run his race that night. It wasn't till the next day," Quist answered for the girl. "Am I right, Rosemary?"

The girl nodded, still fighting tears. Quist crossed over to the bar and made himself a drink. Since the late afternoon of the day now gone, when he had gotten his first look at Ed Smythe with the plastic bag over his head and the car engine pumping death into his lungs, he had been pulled two ways by his reactions to the situation. He had never met Ed Smythe in life, had nothing to go on but Willie Jacobs's analysis of the man, but he'd found himself willing to believe that Smythe could have killed Judith Cameron if he saw she was about to reveal a ringer scandal. But he hadn't been able to buy the torturing of the horse to cover the crime. Not realistic? A man who would shoot a woman in cold blood wouldn't harm a horse? Willie's almost loving picture of a man who cared deeply for horses had stuck with him, enough to make him consider the possibility that Ed Smythe's suicide wasn't connected with Judith's death. The suicide was an easy out for Captain Mowery. "It's a confession," Mowery had said. Smythe knew about the gun and had access to it; the horse couldn't have been a ringer without Smythe knowing; his career, his whole life, would have been over if Judith Cameron had the goods on him. But wouldn't Ed Smythe, animal lover, with only a few brief minutes in which to try to cover his crime, have instinctively taken some other way than torturing the horse?

Now this intense young girl, blotting at her eyes with Kleenex Lydia had produced for her, had added a whole new dimension to the case. A piece of forty-seven million dollars suggested something far bigger than a sixty-to-one ringer winning a stake race.

Quist brought his drink with him from the bar and sat down again, facing Rosemary.

"What did you do, Rosie, after Ed Smythe kicked you out of his cottage that morning?" he asked.

"I—I walked along the beach," she said. "It was all so unreal, that talk about millions of dollars. I was hurt that he hadn't wanted me to stay and help him get pulled together. I was puzzled that a man who didn't drink could have chosen to get himself so very drunk."

"Trying to blot something out," Quist said.

She nodded. "I knew that must be it. I was also hurt that he wouldn't let me help him with whatever it was. We had always been so close. He had always shared his troubles with me—troubles with women, his gambling debts, what he had to do to get untangled from the loan sharks."

"I understand Jerry Carpenter sometimes bailed him out."

"When it got bad," Rosemary said. "Mr. Carpenter liked Ed, knew how valuable he was at his job. It was worth his while to help Ed out of a jam." She shook her head from side to side. "Ed was never in the kind of money trouble that would bother Mr. Carpenter. A few hundred dollars. The loan sharks might get tough if Ed didn't pay up, but a few hundred dollars was nothing to Mr. Carpenter."

"But over a period of time that could add up to something," Quist said.

"I remember the day I saw Ed off to South America," Rosemary said. "He was so keen about going, so high on everything. 'I hope I strike oil down there,' he said. 'Would you believe I'm into Jerry Carpenter about sixteen hundred bucks?' He wasn't worried about it. He was just dreaming about coming back with enough to clear that slate."

" 'A piece of forty-seven million' would take care of that pretty handily," Quist said.

"I just have to believe that was crazy talk," Rosemary said.

"So you walked along the beach."

"I had a horse to exercise—Clothilda," Rosemary said. "I told myself that when Ed really sobered up he'd tell me what was bothering him."

"You weren't afraid?"

"For Ed? Yes. Drinking like that. Something had to be very wrong."

"Afraid for yourself," Quist said. " 'They' would be dangerous if 'they' thought he'd told you something. That didn't bother you?"

She gave Quist a wide-eyed look. "Not then," she said. "I thought it was all part of the crazy hangover talk. So much happened that day. I did my chores with my horse. When I brought her in to cool out, Ed was at work. He and Ben Diamond were getting King Lear ready to truck over to Aqueduct for the race that afternoon. I went over to talk to them and to pat King, who was a friend of mine. Ed looked at me as if he didn't know me, but he knew me well enough to send me into town on an errand—a supply of bandage material he used on the horses. When I got back, he and Ben Diamond and the King were gone."

" 'Not then,' you said. You weren't afraid then about 'they.' "

"I didn't even think about it then," Rosemary said. "But I wanted to be alone with Ed again, try to get him to straighten out all that wild talk. I knew he wouldn't be back till after the afternoon's racing was over at Aqueduct. I had chores, working with some of the other horses. I mean, it was just like any other day. I worked around, and then in the late afternoon we heard about King Lear. He'd won his race and set a new track record for a mile and a furlong. We couldn't believe it, but we were delighted, of course. I waited for Ed and Ben Diamond to bring the horse back, but it was only Ben when the truck came. I asked about Ed. 'celebrating, I guess!' Ben said. 'This crazy bastard'—and he meant the King—'has either got him celebrating or drowning his sorrows, because he didn't have a nickel on him.' "

"You didn't think anything about a ringer then?"

"No. I was just worried about Ed. If he was celebrating with his new fondness for hard stuff, I was worried about him."

"You hear any talk about a ringer?"

"Oh, there was some joking talk. Must have been a ringer because King Lear was really a dog."

"But you didn't wonder, even after Ed's talk about selling out?"

"It just never occurred to me, Julian. Honest racing was Ed's life. Yes, he said he'd sold out. But I knew it couldn't be horses."

"You didn't find Ed where he was celebrating?"

"No. I kept expecting he might show up at the Stirrup Cup, there at the Complex. But he didn't. I finally went home to bed."

"Where do you stay?"

"There's a rooming house in the village. A Mrs. Larson runs it. She lets out two or three rooms to girls who work at the Complex—a waitress, a girl who works at the office of someone, me. Ed found Mrs. Larson's for me."

"So you went to bed."

"I'm due at the track to exercise at six in the morning. Mrs. Larson has coffee and maybe doughnuts or something before I go. When I got to the track all hell had broken loose. Mrs. Cameron was dead and the place was crawling with troopers. I was told that Ben Diamond and Ed were with the police. I heard Ben Diamond's story from people there. I waited for Ed to show up, but he never did. Ben told me the police had let them both go and that Ed had taken off somewhere in his car. I waited around all day. And then the news came that he'd been found—by you and Willie Jacobs. The way you found him—"

Tears reappeared. Quist waited.

"After a long time, long after dark, I saw Willie go into the Stirrup Cup. The place was crowded with people, all talking about the murder of Mrs. Cameron and Ed's suicide. I got Willie aside and he told me how you and he had found Ed. He told me what the cops thought, that Ed was a murderer and a horse torturer. I just couldn't believe that. I told Willie about Ed being drunk, and what he'd told me. Willie said there was just one person who could help me. You, Julian. He said you didn't believe what the cops were saying either."

"True," Quist said. "And I'm a very persistent kind of a guy, Rosie. 'Not then,' you said. You weren't afraid of the people Ed Smythe referred to as 'they' when the day began. But 'not then' suggests you began to be afraid sometime later."

"Willie Jacobs seemed to take it seriously," Rosemary said. "The minute I told him about Ed's ravings, he acted almost scared himself. He kept looking around and looking around. The Stirrup Cup was crowded, people at tables and at the bar. Willie and I were talking in a little alcove near the coat room. I wasn't dressed to go into the main place—work clothes. 'It should seem natural enough for you to be talking to me,' Willie said. 'I did find Ed.' Then he fixed those shrewd little eyes on me. 'I think you shouldn't take what Ed said to you as sauce talk. If it's what I think it is, there are people who would knock you off without any more thought than swatting a fly—if they thought Ed had talked too much to you.' 'But he didn't!' I said. 'Maybe enough,' Willie said, 'because you've got me thinking. I wish you hadn't decided to contact me in such a public place. Someone may think that I know something that you know from talking to Ed.' He looked real worried, Julian."

"Willie doesn't scare easily," Quist said.

"Well, he was uncomfortable anyway," Rosemary said. "I asked him where I could find you. He didn't want to tell me at first. 'You're like Typhoid Mary, kid,' he said. 'A carrier. They think you've got the disease of knowledge from Ed, and anyone you talk to—particularly anyone like Mr. Quist who's publicly interested in the case—may get that same disease from you. Too much knowledge is a dangerous thing, they say.' 'But I don't know anything,' I told him. 'You'd be a hell of a lot safer if there was some way to convince them of that. Maybe I'd be safer, too. And if I tell you where you can find Julian Quist, you got to promise me you won't lead somebody there. If you notice anyone following you—and *look* for it—you go climb the Empire State Building and enjoy the view.' "

Quist's eyes had narrowed. In the world of the horse, Willie Jacobs wasn't someone to shy at phantoms. "You drove in from the Complex in a car?" he asked.

She nodded. "I have a little Volkswagen I use to ferry me around. It was really Ed's, but he let me have it for the summers."

"So did you follow Willie's advice, look for someone tailing you?"

"Yes. And—and when you think something may be going to happen, you imagine it's happening. I thought there were headlights following me when I left the Stirrup Cup. I drove all around the village—main street, back streets. I lost them, I thought. Then on the thruway coming in I thought one pair of headlights stayed right close behind me. I'd speed up and he'd stay close, I'd slow down and he wouldn't pass. I was sure then, and I was suddenly really scared. I cut off the East River Drive uptown somewhere. I thought he was still with me. I drove all around, down one street, up another. Finally I was certain I'd shaken him, and I came here. I parked the car about a block away and waited a good twenty minutes for someone to show an interest in me. Nothing. So I came here."

Quist put down his drink and stood up, stretching his long legs. He gave Rosemary a wry little smile. "So you got to see me under false pretenses."

"But Julian, I—"

"You said you were sure you knew who'd murdered Judith Cameron," Quist said. "It turns out you have no idea, except that it is probably someone Ed Smythe called 'they.' "

*

You either accepted Rosemary Wilson's story as being the truth as she knew it, or a complete fabrication designed, for some reason, to divert Quist from the direction in which he was headed.

"Which is nowhere," he said to Lydia. They were alone for a moment. Rosemary had requested the use of the john and a chance to repair the damage of tears. "I doubted that Ed Smythe would torture a horse. Outside of that I was not headed anywhere."

"And now?" Lydia asked.

"The wild blue yonder of little Miss Wilson's story," Quist said. " 'They,' for God sake. That's where I'm headed!"

"If she was followed here, Julian, and they know that she came here to see you, you can't turn her out into the night at this hour."

"I'm just an innocent and attractive young public relations expert," he said. "Why should that disturb them?"

"Because 'they' can probably read," Lydia said. "You've had a good deal more publicity about your involvement in crime fighting in the last few years than you have as a P.R. man. 'They,' if they aren't blind, must know that you spent a good part of yesterday with Willie Jacobs. The girl, who they think may be dangerous to them, tracks down Willie, who sends her hotfooting it into the city to find you. That should be enough to make them wonder if Rosie and Willie Jacobs and you know more than is good for you."

"But we don't know anything."

"They don't know that, because they have no way of knowing how much Ed Smythe told Rosie before he stuck his head in a plastic bag and turned on his car motor."

"As it turns out, he told her both too much and too little," Quist said. He crossed over to the bar and picked up the house phone. After a moment or two the night man answered. "George? The young lady you brought up here awhile ago—she drove here in a Volkswagen that she says she parked about a block away, I don't know in which direction. Will you see if you can locate it for me?"

"Sure, Mr. Quist."

"And George, I'm not interested in the Volkswagen, but in anyone else who seems to be interested—a car parked nearby, or cruising the neighborhood. Anybody just hanging around watching it. I think someone may have followed the young lady here."

"I get it, Mr. Quist."

"Take your time, George. If someone's moving around, you may not spot them right away. If it's a car, get the license number."

"I'll let you know, Mr. Quist."

Rosemary came back from the john. "I've taken enough of your time," she said.

"You've only just started to take my time, Rosie," Quist said. "Lydia will fix up the guest room for you. I'm not letting you leave here till we have a little better idea who and what we're dealing with."

A look of relief spread over the tired young face. "Oh, Julian, I *was* afraid to go back there by myself."

"Try to get some sleep," Quist said. "I'm going to need you bright and alert in the morning."

Lydia took the girl up to the second floor guest room and Quist went to the outside phone on the bar. He dialed a number from memory. A sleepy voice said, "Hello."

"Mark? It's Julian."

"Would you believe I've been waiting for you to call all night?" the sleepy voice asked.

The voice belonged to Lieutenant Mark Kreevich of the Manhattan Homicide squad. Circumstances had made close friends of these two dissimilar men. Kreevich was a slim, wiry man, with bright blue eyes and an intense manner. He was the new breed of cop, college educated with a law degree. He was dedicated to law and order, but not the cliché kind that politicians talk about in election years. He believed people should be able to live in some other way than on the defensive. He believed that there should be a system in which crime was prevented, not solved after it was committed. He was a cultivated man. He could talk about art and music and literature and the theater. But his mind was never far from the case he was involved with, or cases in which he wasn't involved that taught him things about his profession. Accidentally crime had brought him together with Quist, and they had become a sort of mutual admiration society.

"You've been getting your name in the papers, Buster," Kreevich said. "My mother always said—"

"I know what your mother said, and it isn't for polite society to hear."

"Your ball park, the Complex," Kreevich said. "A murdered lady, a suicidal horse handler, maybe a ringer scandal. With all that material you could write a comic strip for years."

"If you don't stop making jokes, it may take years for me to bring you up-to-date."

"Sorry," Kreevich said, detecting a slight edge to his friend's voice. "Particularly sorry to hear about Judith Cameron. She and Dan Garvey bought me dinner one night out at the Stirrup Cup. Delightful lady. How is Dan bearing up? They looked serious."

"Afraid they were. I haven't seen Dan since yesterday noon. And of course he's bulling around somewhere, trying to find someone to punish."

"As are you, in your own way," Kreevich said. "The

Complex is out of my jurisdiction, Julian. I don't know how I can help you."

"As a friend, not a cop."

"Well, sure!"

"So don't ask questions until I've finished," Quist said. He took it from the top, from an unlikely horse race to the gory death of Judith Cameron, to the suicide of the big man who loved horses, to the visit of that man's illegitimate daughter and wild talk about a sellout and forty-seven million dollars, and "they."

"My turn?" Kreevich asked, when Quist slowed down.

"Go," Quist said.

"You'll get mad if I tell you you're a sentimental slob," the detective said. "Willie Jacobs and your Rosemary tot sing love songs about Ed Smythe and horses. You listen and you decide Smythe couldn't have killed Judith because he couldn't have tortured a horse. How did the old song go? 'Put it all together it spells MOTHER!'? The man gets himself involved in a crooked horse race, is about to be exposed by the lady, his whole career at stake. He's now not Ed Smythe but a demented psychotic. He has to cover himself, and he does it the best way at hand: by turning the horse into a pain-crazed destruction machine. This isn't the Ed Smythe Willie and the girl described to you. This is an Ed Smythe suddenly off his rocker, who won't act or react the way you'd expect him to."

"So you think—?"

"I think that's probably how it was, Julian. But there is another old, old story, chum, we've talked about many times. The man who pulls the trigger isn't necessarily the real criminal. The hitman is just a machine, paid for and directed by someone else. So let's say Ed Smythe killed Judith Cameron and tortured a horse. But—and it's a big but, Julian—who drove him to it? Who are 'they'? And forty-seven million bucks? There's only one kind of crime I know of—except multinational corporate skulduggery—that runs into that kind of money."

"Drugs?"

"Right on," Kreevich said. "And just in passing, you do know, don't you, that a large percentage of illegal drugs that gets into this country comes from South America? And didn't Ed Smythe spend two months in South America this past winter and spring, nursing Jerry Carpenter's horses? We don't believe in coincidences, do we, Julian, but maybe this one is worth looking at."

The little red button on the house phone blinked on and off.

"Hold it a minute, Mark," Quist said, and picked up the house phone.

George, the doorman, was on the other end. "You were right, Mr. Quist. There are a couple of guys in a black Mercury Zephyr who are real interested in the Volkswagen. They're parked down the block, and every few minutes they drive up and have a look at our front door."

"You get a license number, George?"

"New York AJ 197," George said.

"Thanks, George. I'll take it from here," Quist said. He went back to Kreevich on the other phone and reported George's findings. "Those two guys are in your jurisdiction, Mark."

"Hang up. I'll get back to you," Kreevich said.

Quist sat very still for a moment, the palms of his hands pressed against his closed eyelids. It was almost twenty-one hours ago that Vic Lorch had called from the Complex to tell him what had happened to Judith Cameron, and that Dan Garvey had been notified and was already on his way. Quist himself had been on the go ever since, without a moment's letup. He had to quit, to lie down, to close his eyes. But not just yet; not till Mark Kreevich assured him that the men in the Mercury Zephyr were covered and not dangerous to Rosemary or to himself and Lydia. If they believed that Rosemary knew from Ed Smythe what the score was, then anyone the girl had talked to could also be a target. Quist himself, Lydia, and, of course, Willie Jacobs.

In a small book of telephone numbers Quist found the one for the security office at the Complex. Someone manned the phone there around-the-clock, but unfortunately Vic Lorch wasn't on duty. The man who answered gave Quist Lorch's home phone, but Vic didn't respond to a persistent ringing. Bastard is probably shacked up somewhere with a doll, Quist thought.

One other line of thought kept him from falling asleep where he sat. Where was Dan Garvey? Dan had taken off from his office around noon, after their talk, to put the heat on Ben Diamond, whose story of the screaming woman and the enraged King Lear had been accepted by Captain Mowery. Garvey had never checked back or reported on his encounter with Diamond. He seemed to have disappeared for the last fifteen hours. It wasn't entirely out of character for Dan. Quist could imagine the fierce anger that was driving his friend. All Dan was caring about at the moment was catching up with the person responsible for Judith's death. "Drive him into the ground like a fence post," Garvey had said. He would run any risks, no matter how illogical, to do just that. Quist wished he could get in touch with Garvey to give him Rosemary Wilson's story. "They" suggested more than one fence post. Garvey, searching for one man, could find himself surrounded by a small army. If Kreevich's guess was at all accurate, drugs suggested an organization, a group of criminals—the Syndicate, the Mafia, any name you like. One man alone, walking into that kind of power, could find his neck on the chopping block before he had a chance to guess what he was up against.

The phone rang. It was Kreevich.

"You can go to bed now, which I imagine you need to do," the Homicide man said. "The two men in the black Mercury are covered. They'll be picked up presently for loitering."

"Thanks, Mark."

I think the license number may fascinate you," Kreevich said. "AJ 197 is registered to J. D. Carpenter."

"Jerry Carpenter?"

"One and the same," Kreevich said. "He has half a dozen cars licensed in his name. AJ 197 is one of them. Don't grab for the phone, chum. I called Carpenter's home on the South Shore. A sleepy and very annoyed houseman was finally persuaded to wake Carpenter and put him on."

"He was there?"

"Just tumbled in from a long night at the Stirrup Cup," Kreevich said. "Dozens of people can testify he was there. Perfect alibi. This guy is so rich, Julian, he has only a vague idea what he owns. Hasn't the faintest idea what the license numbers of any of his cars are. But he thinks, mind you he *thinks,* there's a Mercury Zephyr used by the stable crew. That includes Hank Benson, his trainer, the unfortunately late Ed Smythe, Ben Diamond, anyone who needs a car for stable business. He has no idea why anyone should be driving it around New York at three thirty in the morning."

"You told him—?"

"I told him nothing, chum. Just that a squad car was about to pick up the driver and his companion for loitering. Gave him the courtesy of putting in a word for them before we made an arrest. He says he has no idea who has the car or why. He'll bail out whoever it is, of course, if they're his people. The car, he suggested, might have been stolen by strangers. In which case he's grateful to us for finding it."

"That is possible, I suppose."

"Well, I'm about to have a long and detailed conversation with them," Kreevich said. "I'll let you know. Get some sleep, or you won't know which end is up by breakfast time."

2

Quist opened his eyes. Sunlight streaming through the windows almost blinded him. He realized he was lying on his side of the king-size bed, his bed and Lydia's. She was sitting on the edge by him, and her fingers felt cool against his cheek.

"I'm sorry to do this to you, love," she said. "But it's almost nine o'clock."

He sat bolt upright. "Good God, Lydia, I should be at—"

"You needed sleep," she said. "But Mark Kreevich just called. He said to call him at his office when you're not cross-eyed. No hurry."

"The girl?" Quist asked.

"Still dead to the world down the hall. I brought you coffee." She pointed to a china mug on the bedside table.

"Angel," he said, and reached out to touch her. The coffee tasted marvelous. "No word from Dan?"

"Nothing."

"Damn him! He must know we're sweating him out."

"Could it be he's walked into something?"

"It could be, love. It could damn well be." He climbed out

of bed, naked. "You think a couple of poached eggs on toast are in the cards?"

"Ten minutes?"

"Perfect. And I think you'd better call Rosie. We've got to work something out for her."

That first cup of coffee, the shave and shower, breakfast and the first slim, black cigar were necessary to launch Quist on a new day. He was just ready for the day when Rosemary Wilson, looking a little tousled and still sleepy, joined him. She was wearing one of Lydia's negligees which was too long for her. She looked, he thought, like a very young child.

"Feed the lady something, Lydia, while I get on to Kreevich," Quist said. "I need to know what I'm going to do with you, Rosie."

Kreevich sounded brisk and businesslike when Quist got him at his office.

"Did you know," he asked Quist, "that a very high-class call girl lives around the corner from you in one of those old brownstones?"

"It's the neighborhood for it," Quist said.

"Two young men who work around the Complex were trying to find the lady last night. Her name is Claire Kingman. She was evidently out on call—they say. The night watchman at Carpenter's stables at the Complex, one Bull Teliski, is the father of Pete Teliski, one of the two young men. The other one's name is Pat Grogan. They wanted—they say—to find the Kingman girl. Papa Teliski told them they could borrow Carpenter's Mercury provided they'd gas it up before they brought it back—they say. Papa Teliski verifies that. They know who Rosemary Wilson is, but they had no interest in her—they say. Didn't follow her into town—they say."

"You sound like a stuck record. They say!"

"Because I don't believe a damned word of it," Kreevich

said. "Why would they be waiting around the corner, out of sight of the Kingman girl's building, if they were waiting for her to come home?"

"You asked them?'-

"Of course I asked them. She always comes home along Beekman Place—they say."

"And she says?"

"She still hasn't come home," Kreevich said. "Long night. But—and I have to concede this—if the lady usually comes home in a taxi . . . Well, even-numbered streets are eastbound, so the driver would cross Fiftieth Street to Beekman Place, turn north on Beekman—the very block where your Miss Wilson's Volkswagen is parked and where Teliski and Grogan were sitting around in the Mercury—and then west on Fifty-first to the Kingman doll's brownstone. Why they would wait on Beekman Place to spot the lady in a taxi and not on Fifty-first where she'd get out at her front door is not entirely clear to me, but it could hold some water."

"If she had a guy with her, they didn't want to be seen," Quist suggested.

"So your doorman, George, tells you that they cruised up Beekman in that Mercury, showing an interest in your front door, chum. Students of modern architecture, you think?"

"No."

"Too many coincidences, Julian. They are connected, through Papa Teliski, with Carpenter. They work at the Complex, Peter Teliski as a counterman in the food concession, Grogan as an electrician in plant maintenance. They know Rosemary by sight. They knew Ed Smythe, of course—Papa's friend and fellow worker. You want to buy as a coincidence that Rosemary talks to Willie Jacobs in the Stirrup Cup, gets in her Volkswagen and heads for you on Beekman Place at exactly the same moment that young Teliski and Grogan borrow Carpenter's car, take the same route to Beekman Place, park in the same block, and are interested in your front door? Your Rosemary says when she speeded up they speeded up, when she slowed down they slowed down. More coincidence?"

"I think no," Quist said.

"I had to let them go, of course," Kreevich said. "They had a right to the car—at least Papa Teliski gave them permission to borrow it. Technically they were loitering, but they had a destination. That's the one real coincidence in the whole business, Julian. Rosemary led them to your building, but it happens they had a girl friend who lives just around the corner. Made their story come easy."

"What do I do with Rosemary?" Quist asked.

Kreevich's voice was suddenly harsh. "What do you do with yourself? What do you do with Lydia?" he asked. "If 'they' think Rosemary had some critical information from Ed Smythe that she passed along to Willie Jacobs and to you and Lydia, then you're all under the gun. You heard from Garvey?"

"No."

"Where is the sonofabitch?"

"I wish I knew."

"He could be in the same kind of trouble."

"Could be." Quist drew a deep breath. "I've got to go back to the Complex. That's where the action is."

"Be sure to dress for it," Kreevich said.

"Dress for what?"

"Someone taking a shot at you from behind a tree, or a barn, or the next booth in the men's room. You'd want to look nice in the morgue, wouldn't you? Lydia and Rosemary aren't worth protecting?"

Kreevich wasn't a man to try to scare you for the fun of it. The Homicide man was convinced that there was real danger. The angry note in his voice reflected his frustration at not being able to offer direct help.

Quist rejoined Lydia and Rosemary. The girl had just finished the breakfast Lydia had prepared for her. Quist sat down at the table, frowning at the mug of coffee Lydia brought him.

"It seems, Rosie," he said, "that the two men George saw hanging around outside last night are people you know. Peter Teliski and Pat Grogan."

"Oh, wow!" Rosemary said.

"You do know them?"

"Of course. Pete Teliski is Bull Teliski's son. Bull is our night watchman in Shed Row. Pete works for the food concession people. Pat's in maintenance, an electrician I think. He and Pete are close friends, always together in off-hours. Ed—Ed didn't think much of either of them."

"Why?"

"Irresponsible, he thought. He used to say you couldn't count on today's young people. He thought they cared more about their personal fun than their job."

"But you know these two?"

"Yes."

"Friends?"

Rosemary's eyes lowered. "They think I'm still just a kid," she said.

"They say they came to see a girl who lives around the corner from here," Quist said. "But they surely followed you, love."

She looked up. "Why?"

"Did you notice whether either of them were in the Stirrup Cup when you were talking to Willie Jacobs last night?"

The girl shook her head, slowly. "The place was crowded, Julian. I wasn't interested in anyone but Willie, I didn't notice anyone I knew, except Jerry Carpenter, who was there with a party. Why would they follow me?"

"Because they think Ed Smythe may have told you something about 'they,'" Quist said. "Now they think you told Willie, and that you certainly told me and Lydia. Lieutenant Kreevich of Homicide thinks we're all in danger."

"Do you, Julian?" Lydia asked.

"I don't think we should laugh it off as a joke," Quist said. "I'm going out to the Complex to try to locate Dan and to warn Willie Jacobs. I want you two to stay here in the apartment. Don't let anyone in, not even God, till I get back."

"I've got to go to the office, Julian," Lydia said. "With you and Dan out, the place will be a madhouse."

"Bobby and Connie are going to have to handle it," Quist said. Bobby Hilliard, who looked like a shy young Jimmy Stewart, was one of the associates, a genius at handling temperamental people. Connie Parmalee, a tall girl with coppery red hair and grey-green eyes behind tinted, wire-rimmed granny glasses, was Quist's fabulous secretary. "An emergency has the three of us out of the office, and that's that," Quist continued. "The day doorman will protect you from down below. Double lock the door up here. And unless it's me, there's nobody home. Don't answer the phone. If I want to call, I'll let it ring twice, hang up, and call again."

"Suppose Dan is trying to reach you?"

"He'll have sense enough to know I'm at the Complex looking for him."

Lydia followed Quist to the apartment vestibule.

"What do I do if Rosemary doesn't want to stay?" she asked, her arm slipped through his.

"Charm her," Quist said. "If that doesn't work, lock her

in the john. She's in more trouble than any of us, love."

"Don't kid me, Julian. How serious is it?"

He took her by the shoulders and looked down at her steadily. "If Ed Smythe wasn't having an opium dream, it's forty-seven million dollars serious. If anyone thinks we can wreck that kind of deal, we aren't good insurance risks." He bent down and kissed her. "Play it cool, darling."

"Julian! What about you?"

"You play it safe, love. Dan and Willie Jacobs have got to be told what they're up against. If the situation was reversed, they'd both try to warn us."

A summer day, warm, with a faint breeze blowing in off the river. The garage where Quist kept his car was just around the corner, only one hundred and fifty yards from the front door of his apartment building. In that short walk every instinct he had for danger seemed to be alerted. He could have sworn someone was watching him. He could feel the short hairs on the back of his neck rising. He stopped three or four times to look around, but he couldn't see anyone who appeared to be following him. Kid stuff, being afraid of something that wasn't there, he told himself. But he walked faster and felt a sense of relief when he stepped into the garage and waited for the elevator to bring down his car from an upper floor. In his time Quist had known danger, but he had almost always been certain where it was coming from, could put a face to the enemy. "They" had no faces, except two young men whom Kreevich had turned loose because he had nothing on them. To Quist those two were still blanks, but he would catch up with them when he reached the Complex.

The drive out to the Island wasn't comfortable. He kept his eyes on the rear-view mirror. Once he convinced himself that a small sports convertible was adjusting its speed to his, keeping a few car lengths behind. He tried speeding up and was satisfied that the sports car also picked up speed. He slowed down and moved over to the right lane, and the little car shot past him. False alarm. Or was the driver satisfied that Quist was headed for the Complex and didn't want to arouse suspicion? Quist's hands felt damp on the wheel of his car.

The drive seemed longer than usual, but finally it came to an end. Quist parked outside the Arena Building, got out, and looked around. No sign of the little sports car anywhere. Old woman, Quist told himself.

He went into the security office in search of Vic Lorch and found the big man there. Forty-seven million dollars. Who did you trust with that kind of money on the line? Perhaps not even your best friend.

"Tried to call you last night without any luck," Quist said.

Lorch grinned at him. "Do I have to ask your permission to shack up with a doll? I found a message that you'd called and I tried to reach you at your apartment awhile back but I guess you were already on your way."

At least Lydia wasn't answering the phone, as she'd promised.

"Dan been in touch with you?" Quist asked.

Lorch looked genuinely concerned. "No. Haven't you heard from him?"

"Nothing."

"Crazy bastard trying to handle things all by himself," Lorch said. "This thing looks pretty open-and-shut to me, Julian. Ed Smythe got himself caught up in this ringer deal, killed Mrs. Cameron when she caught him out, tried to cover it by damaging the horse, and then couldn't stand it and did himself in."

"You know his daughter?"

"Rosie? Sure. Nice kid. She must be taking this pretty

hard. I've looked around for her, thinking I might be able to do something to help. But nobody's seen her since last night. She's always here to work a couple of horses, but not this morning."

"Who would she turn to with Ed gone?" Quist asked, knowing the answer.

"Mrs. Larson, in the boardinghouse where she lives. But I called the old lady, and she said Rosie hadn't come home last night."

"Have you seen Willie Jacobs around?"

"Not this morning. What did you call me about last night, Julian?"

"Looking for Dan," Quist said. A new world where you weren't sure of old friends. If Lorch knew where Rosemary was, he might let it slip. But that, too, was a little absurd. Teliski and Grogan knew where she was.

"A couple of kids from out here were picked up hanging around my place last night," Quist said. "Peter Teliski and Pat Grogan. Cops turned them loose when they said they were waiting for some call girl who lives in my neighborhood. The officer in charge checked with me because he knew I had contacts out here." So much for truth.

"A couple of crazy creeps, those two," Lorch said. "I've been trying for months to get them off the grounds, fired from their jobs. I'm the chief villain in their lives."

"How come?"

"On the surface, they're just plain irresponsible hell-raisers. Below the surface I've suspected they've been peddling drugs on the lot, but I haven't been able to prove it. I've tried to set them up with a couple of undercover people, trying to get them to make a sale. No dice. Out here, Julian, we're very big on the be-kind-to-ex-servicemen jazz. Both those kids fought in Vietnam, which is probably where they first got into drugs. But we don't fire them, the management tells me, just because they're a little 'wild.' After all, they fought for their country."

Quist sat very still, staring at the big man across the desk from him. Vic Lorch was an ex-cop. When the management, backed by a group of young millionaires who put up most of the money for the Complex, had been looking for someone to handle security, Quist had gone to his police connections in the city, Kreevich among them. Someone had recommended Lorch, who wanted out from police routines. Kreevich didn't know Lorch then, but he vouched for his record. Since then they had met when the Manhattan detective had gone to some of the events at the Arena with Quist. Lorch had apparently been first-rate at his job from the very start.

Quist didn't see himself as a lonely hero on a white charger. Unlike Garvey, he was a realist. If he was up against an organized mob of some sort, he would be an idiot to play the game solo. Maybe no one could be trusted with a piece of forty-seven million dollars dangled in front of him, but if Lorch was on the level he was the best possible person to be helpful.

"If you wanted to polish me off, Vic, I'd be a fool to hand you a loaded gun, wouldn't I?" Quist said.

"One of my problems with the Police Department was that I was a little too quick on the draw," Lorch said, cheerfully. "I'm not supposed to be a good man with a loaded gun." And then he realized that Quist hadn't been joking. "What the hell are you talking about, Julian?"

"If it was just me I wouldn't hesitate to take the chance," Quist said. "But there are others."

"Will you knock it off and tell me what you're hinting at?" Lorch was a little angry, and it sounded in his voice.

"I still don't buy the Ed Smythe story just the way Captain

Mowery has it written off," Quist said. "Ed Smythe did some talking before he died."

"To you and Willie Jacobs? I thought—"

"He talked about selling out," Quist said. "He talked about 'a piece of forty-seven million dollars.' Enough to keep him out of trouble for the rest of his life."

"You're kidding! "

"I've talked to Mark Kreevich about it," Quist said. "He suggested drugs. He suggested South America where Smythe recently spent two months. He suggested a sellout to some kind of organization or mob or Syndicate. He suggested that those of us who knew what Ed said before he died could be in big trouble."

Lorch's face had gone hard. "And you think I might be a member of a mob that's out to get you?"

"Or I've put you on the spot by telling you," Quist said.

"So you better tell it all," Lorch said.

Quist took a deep breath and let it out in a long sigh. If Lorch was a friend, he needed him. If he was an enemy, he already knew about Rosemary, where she was, what she must have told. A friend needed the facts. An enemy already had them, except the fact that Ed Smythe had revealed almost nothing. He had talked about a sellout, about "they," but nothing that pointed to any particular person or group.

Quist told it all.

Lorch listened, sitting like a stone statue behind his desk. A cigarette burned out in the ashtray beside him.

"My problem," Quist said, when he had finished with the facts, "is that with so much money involved—forty-seven million dollars—almost anybody could be bought off, the very best of people. The right amount of money, the right woman, can tempt any man."

"Maybe so," Lorch said, after a moment, "but all I can

tell you, Julian, is that nobody has made me an offer. Maybe if they did I would fall for it, but no one has."

Quist tried smiling. His face felt stiff. "I must believe in you, Vic, or I'd have kept my mouth shut."

Lorch leaned forward and held out his hand across the desk. Quist took it in a firm handshake.

"I'm glad Kreevich is in on it," Lorch said. "The center of any kind of mob operation is certain to be in the city, his ball park, and not out here."

"And yet the fringes of it are here," Quist said. "Smythe, Ben Diamond, the two Teliskis and Pat Grogan, maybe Hank Benson. Can you guess where the ringer horse comes into the picture?"

"Penny-ante stuff compared to the kind of money you've been talking about," Lorch said. "Yet Smythe, if he wasn't dreaming when he talked to Rosie, seems to have touched two different bases." He fished in his shirt pocket for a cigarette. "Where do you want to go from here?"

"The first thing I want is to locate Dan and Willie Jacobs and let them know what we think they're up against."

"I'll spread the word," Lorch said. "My men can find them if they're anywhere here at the Complex."

Quist reached for the phone on Lorch's desk and dialed his own number on Beekman Place. He let it ring twice, disconnected, and then dialed again. After three rings Lydia answered.

"All quiet?" he asked her.

"The phone has rung a couple of times but I didn't answer because it wasn't your signal," Lydia said. "The temptation to answer is enormous, Julian."

"Resist it," Quist said. "If it's Dan he'll have sense enough to try me out here eventually."

"He may have tried the office. If you haven't checked in there they must be going crazy—no you, no Dan, no me."

"I'll check," Quist said. "Love you."

"Please take care, Julian. You matter to too many of us."

Connie Parmalee, Quist's secretary, sounded calm and unrattled when he got through to her. Like so many young women in her position, Connie was unashamedly in love with the man she worked for, but there was never anything in her contact with him to suggest it. If not for Lydia she might have gone gunning for him quite openly.

"I'm at the Complex," Quist told her.

"I listen to the radio," Connie said.

"I'm trying to locate Dan. He hasn't checked in?"

"Nor Lydia. Is she with you?"

"Things are on the sticky side, Connie. I know where Lydia is, quite safe. But Dan has evaporated somewhere. If he calls, tell him to try me at the security office at the Complex. The number is—"

"I have the number," Connie said. "I've shifted half a dozen appointments lined up for you."

"Keep the floorboards nailed down," Quist said.

The Complex had become, overnight, a setting for violence and crime. But the paths in the shade of the trees that graced Shed Row and the racetrack area itself—the special world of the horse, as Willie Jacobs called it—seemed undisturbed by the bloody death of Judith Cameron, the slaughter of King Lear, the grim suicide of Ed Smythe. Horses were being led along the shady paths, stood outside their stalls being curried and brushed and rubbed down by grooms. Others, watched over by stable boys, cropped at the green grass that had cost thousands to plant and grow. In a concrete and macadam world it was a peaceful, lush oasis. People may have been talking about the violence that had shocked the place, but the quiet, almost graceful routines were undisturbed. There were horses being readied for the day's racing across the Island at Aqueduct, others being prepared for next month's meeting at Saratoga. Dogs moved around as if the property was theirs. The old belief that a frightened horse will follow a goat out of a burning stable resulted in a healthy goat population. Near the stables you were conscious of the aroma of saddle soap and expensive tack.

As Willie Jacobs might have put it, ladies and gentlemen perambulated. Willie wouldn't have meant simply men and women who used fancy language, but ladies and gentlemen who had an almost forgotten elegance. They are born, Willie might have said, to wear clothes with a special air. No one has taught them, but they move, like trained actors, with a special style. They can afford the very best materials and the most expensive tailors and designers to make their clothes just so.

"You can spot a fake, an imitator, a mile away," Willie once told Quist. "They can buy their clothes from the same sources but they don't know how to wear them. You can watch a thoroughbred horse and no one told him how to pick 'em and put 'em down. But no other kind of horse moves the same way. It's the same with people who own them and love them. The way they pick 'em and put 'em down is special, even though they can't tell you how they do it."

Into this world of wealth and leisure and charm and tradition, someone had introduced the taint of an evil violence, of greed, of treachery, and, if Kreevich was right about drugs, the means for destroying thousands of lives.

Eleven o'clock in the morning, and Quist wasn't worried about thousands of lives, only two: Dan Garvey and Willie Jacobs. Those two were not strangers to the army of people who worked around the Complex. Garvey had watched every brick put in place on top of every other brick; he had discussed the best ways of doing things and planning things with everyone who had reason to use even the simplest facilities of the plant. He knew everyone from the lowest dishwasher to the fancy maître d' in the Stirrup Cup, from stable hand and exercise boy to owners at the track, from locker room boy to hockey star in the Arena. Dan made a business of being liked. It was important to him in his job. It was unthinkable that if Dan was anywhere on the lot no one could remember seeing him since the day before, the day that Judith Cameron had died. A dozen people had seen him talking to Ben Diamond around noon that day. After that he had simply disappeared from view.

Willie Jacobs's sphere was more limited than Dan's. His was the world of the horse, of Shed Row and the track, of jockeys and timers and touts, of trainers and grooms and exercise kids. Owners knew Willie and enjoyed his colorful language, his unfailing good humor, his shrewd observations about their world. Willie couldn't pass one of them without a wave, a greeting. No one had seen him, or waved, or said hello since the night before, when he had been circulating at the Stirrup Cup. A busboy there remembered seeing him talking to Rosie Wilson, and that was that.

Someone had to be lying about both of them, Quist told himself. Someone had to know where they were and why they continued to stay out of sight. He circulated, asking questions. Vic Lorch's army of security men circulated, asking questions. So far they had all come up empty.

In the wing at Shed Row where Jerry Carpenter's horses were stabled, Quist discovered confusion. The millionaire owner was there along with Hank Benson, the trainer.

"We're unexpectedly shorthanded," Carpenter told Quist. "You know about Ed Smythe. You found him, didn't you? He would normally be in charge here, poor devil. But Ben Diamond hasn't shown up. And Rosie Wilson, old Ed's adopted daughter I think she is, hasn't shown up. She is an exercise rider for us. Not only no show, but no word to anyone. Hank Benson's up the wall trying to find some help."

"Everybody's looking for someone, it seems," Quist said. "I'm trying to find Dan Garvey and Willie Jacobs, and neither one of them seems to be around anywhere."

"Haven't seen either of them," Jerry said. "Hold on. I think I saw Willie in the Stirrup Cup last night."

"He was there," Quist said. "That's the last anyone remembers seeing him. The last anyone remembers seeing Garvey, he was talking to your man Diamond—yesterday, after Judith was killed."

The little crow's-feet tightened at the corners of Jerry's eyes. "You want to buy some horses, Julian? I feel like throwing in the whole ball game. It's never going to be the same again. Judith won't ever come around the corner toward me down here on Shed Row. She won't be on the farm next to mine in Kentucky. And knowing that one of my people was responsible for what happened to her! I don't think I'm going to want to play around with this anymore."

"She wouldn't want you to quit," Quist said.

"Poor darling. She enjoyed living so damned much. And she'd found herself the right man—Dan Garvey."

"I wish I could find him," Quist said.

"He may just have holed up somewhere," Jerry said, "feeling the way he must feel. Have you tried Judith's house down on the South Shore? She had a housekeeper and a secretary there. Dan may have been concerned about them, stayed to help them get things organized. They must all be in shock."

Garvey would want to be helpful to Judith's people, Quist thought, but nothing ordinary would have kept him out of circulation for so long in his search for a killer. Kindness and sympathy weren't out of character for Dan, but once he was aimed at a target nothing could easily divert him. Dan, Quist had to believe, was either on a hot trail or he had fallen into some kind of a trap in the process.

Quist changed directions. "I got caught up in some business of yours in the middle of the night," he said to Carpenter.

"Oh?"

"Policeman friend of mine in the city had picked up a couple of people who work out here. Thought maybe I could vouch for them. One of them was the son of your night watchman, I believe."

"Those crazy goons," Carpenter said, laughing. "Your cop friend got me up in the middle of the night, too. They had a car of mine. Bull Teliski, my night watchman, told them they could borrow it. Woman-chasing, for God sake!"

"You didn't object to their having your car?"

"Not really, as long as they brought it back in one piece. And they did." Carpenter gave Quist a wry little smile. "They could wind up in trouble, though."

"How's that?"

"This is off the record, Julian. The lady they were after, Claire Kingman, is pretty much the private property of someone who can kick them out of their jobs and really burn them if he ever finds out."

"I understand from my police friend that the Kingman broad is a call girl," Quist said.

"With one customer, who pays the rent and keeps her pretty luxuriously. The boys were poaching in posted territory."

Carpenter seemed to be in the mood to share a joke. "The one and only Matthew Boylan."

The board of directors of the Complex were referred to as the Young Millionaires. Matt Boylan—robust, hearty, hard-drinking playboy—was a little long in the tooth to fit that description. Close to sixty, Quist thought, waiting forever to inherit from his father, the steel magnate, who didn't have the sense to call it quits at eighty-four. Quist had dealings with the board, which included Jerry Carpenter. They were primarily sportsmen, spending money for their own pleasure. Their investments in the Sports Complex were more of a tax dodge than a profit venture. They were easy to get along with, enjoying their patterns for living, with the exception of Matt Boylan. Boylan, Quist thought, was a bully who insisted on having his own way, even if he didn't know what he was talking about. He'd been constantly in Quist's hair about public relations for the Complex, his suggestions almost never sensible. He was, Quist knew, married with half a dozen grown children. And, it seemed, a mistress.

"Speak of the devil," Carpenter said.

Coming toward them from between the box stalls on Shed Row were two men. One of them, in a loud checked sports jacket and flamboyant plaid slacks, was Matthew Boylan. The other, a stranger to Quist, was a dark, handsome man with a wide white-toothed smile, wearing a pale sharkskin summer suit with a bright red sports shirt.

"You know Johnny Ricardo?" Carpenter asked Quist.

"No."

"Juan Ricardo. Venezuelan oil tycoon. Horse nut," Carpenter said. "It was through his urging that I sent a string of thoroughbreds to South America last winter. It's always summer where Johnny Ricardo is. I kid him about the possibility that he doesn't own an overcoat. It's never cold where Johnny is."

"Morning, Jerry," Boylan said, in his big voice. He gave Quist an unfriendly glance. "Quist."

"Juan Ricardo, Julian Quist," Carpenter said, making the necessary introduction.

Ricardo gave Quist a firm handshake. His black eyes sparkled. He was a man delighted with the whole world and with every new experience that came his way.

"You are a legend, even where I come from, Mr. Quist," he said. "Julian Quist Associates, I've heard, can turn a black sheep into a knight in shining armor." There was only the faintest tinge of a Spanish accent. Quist imagined a British education.

"Or a knight in shining armor into a black sheep," Matt Boylan said. "What's all this about your not going along with Captain Mowery's solution to the murder of Judith Cameron?"

"Who told you that?" Quist asked.

"Well, naturally I've been in contact with Captain Mowery," Boylan said. "As chairman of the board of directors, it's my responsibility to know what the hell's going on around here. You don't believe this Smythe fellow killed the lady?"

"I don't think there is proof of it yet," Quist said.

"There's proof enough for Mowery," Boylan said, his square chin jutting forward.

"I'm fascinated, Mr. Quist, that you don't agree with the police," Ricardo said. "I got to know Ed Smythe this past winter when he managed Jerry's horses in Buenos Aires." He embraced them all with his smile. "Any man, I always say, can be driven to murder if the pressure is intense enough. But he will not go against his basic character in all ways. When I heard the horse had been tortured, I said to myself, that cannot be Ed Smythe. I've seen him work with horses—pet them, soothe them, plead with them, persuade them. He wasn't a man who got his way with a rough hand.

No, I said to myself, it cannot have been Ed Smythe who tortured that horse."

"Do you have a different candidate, Quist?" Boylan asked.

"Not yet," Quist said quietly.

"So you're just stirring up uncertainty," Boylan said. "Getting us bad publicity when we don't need it. We've got to quash this talk about a ringer. And if you spread the word that the police have been imcompetent—!"

"Right now," Quist said, suppressing his anger, "I'm interested in finding Dan Garvey. Have you seen him anywhere this morning?"

"I suppose he's storming around, threatening people," Boylan said. "No, I haven't seen him."

Quist turned to Jerry Carpenter. "You know where your man Diamond lives?"

"Rooming house somewhere," Carpenter said. "There are hundreds of private homes in the area that take in people who work at the Complex. Hank Benson probably knows."

"Last person known to have talked to Dan," Quist said. "I think I'd like to check it out with him."

Hank Benson, the trainer, wasn't eager for conversation. He was busy giving instructions to two youngsters he'd recruited to fill in for his missing help. He gave Quist the address of a house not far from the track where Diamond boarded. They'd checked there, trying to find him. No luck.

"I haven't seen Dan Garvey around," Benson said, in answer to Quist's second question. "But I noticed his car when I came to work this morning. Red Jaguar, isn't it? It was parked just back of the short-order shack at the head of Shed Row. Garvey must be somewhere nearby."

Quist walked quickly down the alley between the stalls, out into the area fronting Shed Row. Half a dozen men were grouped at the short-order counter, which did a land-office business all day in coffee, sandwiches, doughnuts, and pie. He circled the counter and there, just behind it, was Dan's car. Quist went over to it and felt the radiator. It was stone cold.

The counterman and his customers all had the same answer to Quist's question.

"Dan was here talking to Ben Diamond around noon yesterday," the counterman said. "His car's been there ever since. Not like him to leave it overnight."

"Nobody seen him circulating?"

Nobody had.

The house where Ben Diamond boarded was about a mile from the Complex down Route 14. Quist drove there in his own car. An old man sat in a rocking chair on the front porch, watching the world go by.

"You ain't gonna find Ben here," he told Quist.

"You know where he is?"

"Don't know and ain't gonna know," the old man said. He rubbed at the grey stubble on his chin. "Paid up and took off yesterday afternoon. I figure he didn't want to talk to the cops anymore. Had a roll on him big enough to choke one of his horses. Hank Benson and Bull Teliski been looking for him, but I guess he didn't tell anyone what he was up to or where he was headed. They seemed surprised he was gone."

"You saw him when he came here yesterday?" Quist asked.

"I just told you, didn't I? I took his rent money from him for my daughter."

"He came in a car?"

"Sure. Nobody walks these days. Lot of crazies you see running, but nobody walks to get someplace."

"So Diamond has a car."

"Not a car of his own, if that's what you mean. He'd use a

stable car, or somebody'd drive him home here at night."

"So he had a stable car yesterday?"

"Could be," the old man said. "Fifty years ago I could name any car I saw, tell you the make and the year. Now they all look alike—to me, anyhow."

"Did Diamond always live here?" Quist asked.

"When he was here. He was in South America the last couple of months. They got back about three days ago. He just had to pay me for three days. Went in, got his stuff—which wasn't much—and took off. We'd counted on him for the summer, except August when he'd be in Saratoga."

Quist thanked the old man and turned away.

"Hey, mister!" the old man called after him. "Come to think of it, that was a pickup truck Ben was driving yesterday. Never saw him drive a pickup truck before."

"Well, thanks," Quist said.

"Something loaded in the back under a tarpaulin," the old man said.

"Thanks again."

"Connecticut license plates, blue and white," the old man called out as Quist reached his car.

"You don't remember the numbers?" Quist asked.

"No reason to," the old man said, and settled back in his rocker.

Quist drove back to the Complex and parked outside Lorch's office. Ben Diamond was Dan's last known contact that they knew about. Diamond, wherever he was headed, had a twenty-four-hour start without leaving the faintest suggestion of where to look for him.

Lorch wasn't in his office, but the man covering the phone reported to Quist that Lieutenant Kreevich of Manhattan Homicide was trying to reach him. Kreevich sounded unnaturally tense when he answered the phone.

"Fasten your seat belt," he said.

"What's up?"

"On a side street near the West Side waterfront a patrol car spotted an abandoned Ford pickup truck, no license plates. It was towed away to a pier where we take illegally parked and abandoned cars. Something under a tarpaulin in the back of the truck seemed to be moving. It turned out to be an unconscious man, moaning."

"Ben Diamond!" Quist said.

"I wish it had been," Kreevich said. "It's Dan, Julian."

"My God!"

"He's at St. Vincent's Hospital," Kreevich said. "Intensive care."

"What does he say happened?"

"He doesn't say, Julian, because he's in a coma. He may or may not come out of it. Fractured skull. Until they operate there's no way of telling if there's brain damage."

"What do the doctors say?"

"Fifty-fifty—probably less good than that."

Quist felt as if he'd been slugged. "I've just been talking to someone who saw Ben Diamond driving a pickup truck yesterday afternoon, tarpaulin-covered load in the back, Connecticut license plates. Place where he lived, a mile from here. Diamond paid up, took his stuff, drove off. Could Dan have been in the back of that truck a whole day?"

"I don't have a minute-by-minute medical report," Kreevich said. "Whatever happened to him almost certainly happened out there. But finding him here get's my foot in the door."

"Thank God," Quist said.

"Your faith is touching," Kreevich said, his voice harsh. "I hope it's justified. The doctor at St. Vincent's is William Thomas. I have a man there in case Dan gets able to talk. They tell me that's not likely for hours or even days."

"He must know something, Mark. There could be another try at him in case they know he isn't dead," Quist said.

"Over my dead body," Kreevich said.

It wasn't just a puzzle anymore. It was deeply, hurtfully personal. Dan was as close to Julian as a brother. With death hovering over Dan, the solution to the murder of Judith Cameron and the motives for the suicide of Ed Smythe were, for the moment, secondary in importance. Dan must have everything he needed—the best doctors, the best care. If he came back to consciousness he shouldn't open his eyes and see only an impersonal nurse, Kreevich's bodyguard.

Quist ignored the speed limit driving back into the city, thinking that Dan must have stumbled on answers to Judith's death and Smythe's suicide. What he had discovered had made him a target for "they." Quist convinced himself that Kreevich and the local cops could cover the territory of crime. His job was to be with Dan. He was the one person Dan could surely trust when he was able to talk.

He had almost forgotten the missing Willie Jacobs. Was Willie hidden under a tarpaulin somewhere, or floating in the ocean, because "they" thought he knew too much? It wasn't possible, with Dan in intensive care, to cover all the bases. Dan came first.

Julian had called Lydia before he left Lorch's office. Her impulse was to go straight to St. Vincent's to be with Dan, but Quist had persuaded her that she and Rosemary Wilson should stay where they were till there were more answers. "They" could still be covering everyone who might know too much.

"Including you, Julian," Lydia said.

"I am immortal till I find out who clobbered Dan," he said.

"Oh God, I wish you were, Julian."

"Eyes in the back of my head," he said.

Remembering he'd said that, he kept constantly studying his rear-view mirror as he raced along the thruway into town. As far as he could tell, no one was interested in him, not even a speed cop. It was a time of relatively light traffic in both directions.

It seemed to take forever to find a parking space near the hospital. Finally, inside, it took time to locate Dan. Intensive care was flooded with people brought in off the streets: two Puerto Rican boys screaming with pain from knife wounds received in a gang fight; parents wailing and praying audibly; a heart attack case; the victim of a hit-and-run driver; a woman mugged and beaten in a subway station. No Garvey. Blank looks when Quist asked the question. Everyone seemed to be in a hurry, though quietly efficient. Heart machines beeped away as he'd seen them in the movies. Quist finally cornered an orderly who stayed still long enough to listen to questions. Finally the mention of police rang a bell with him.

"I think the patient you're looking for was moved to a private room. Ask at the desk."

At the desk he was told that Daniel Garvey could not receive visitors. His awareness that there was a policeman with the patient broke the ice a little. A call to Garvey's room got him a clearance from Kreevich's man.

Sergeant Hogan, a plain-clothes detective, had been alerted by Kreevich that Quist would appear. He was a square man with reddish hair and an Irish look to him. He greeted Quist at the door of the room. "I.D., if you don't mind, Mr. Quist."

Quist produced driver's license, credit cards.

A nurse sat beside the bed where Dan lay. Dan's head was swathed in bandages and there was tubing up his nose. The visible part of his face was the color of ashes. His breathing sounded shallow to Quist. The heart machine on the bedside table beeped unevenly. Other tubes, fed from glass bottles, were attached to Dan's arm.

"Have they operated?" Quist asked Hogan.

"Not possible yet," the detective said. "They say he might not survive it. They're trying to fight infection, build him up a little. Before evening, they think."

"He hasn't spoken?"

"Nothing."

"How much do you know about the case?"

"The lieutenant gave me a briefing," Hogan said. "They didn't want to move him out of intensive care, but there are so many unidentified people coming and going, off the street, relatives and friends of patients. We'd have needed an army to make sure of security for your friend."

"The pickup truck where they found Dan," Quist said. "Did they find anything? Fingerprints? Any kind of ownership clue?"

"I'm not getting the word every ten minutes," Hogan said. "Last I heard there was nothing. Fingerprints, but they haven't checked out with anything on record the last I heard. If they had I'd be told who to look for."

"No point in asking you a medical question."

"The word they use is 'critical,' " Hogan said.

"What about Dan's personal belongings?" Quist asked. "I suppose the staff turns them over to the front office." He was thinking that Dan might have written something down, a phone number, an address.

"There were no personal belongings," Hogan said. "He was wearing a seersucker jacket, slacks, the usual shirt, underwear, socks, shoes. But no wallet, no money, no nothing. It was a lucky coincidence that he was identified."

"Coincidence?"

"One of the patrol car cops who stopped to examine the abandoned pickup used to be on special duty at the Stadium when your friend played football. Recognized him. Since it was clearly an attempted homicide, the report was picked up by the lieutenant, a personal friend. Your man had luck all the way. If it hadn't been for that patrol cop remembering him when he played football, he'd be a zero in some hospital about now, unprotected."

"Kreevich agrees with me there may be another attempt to get to him?"

"So he says. If he hadn't alerted me you'd be coming, you wouldn't have got within a mile of here," Hogan said.

Quist walked over to the bed. The nurse stationed there looked hostile.

"I'm his closest friend, business partner," Quist said. "I won't disturb him."

"There's no way you can disturb him," the nurse said. "It's a deep coma."

"Is it possible he could hear me?" Quist asked.

"A miracle," the nurse said.

"It's worth a chance," Quist said. He reached down and covered Dan's exposed left hand with his. "Dan! It's Julian. I'm here when you're ready."

There was no response; not the flicker of an eyelid, nothing. Quist turned at the sound of the room door opening. A doctor in a green hospital gown had come into the room. Hogan was explaining who the visitor was.

"I'm Dr. Thomas," he said. "We've examined the skull X rays, Mr. Quist, and feel we can't wait. Life signs aren't good, but if we don't go in and relieve pressures, he hasn't got a chance."

"He's to have the best of everything, Doctor. Consultation?"

"The best neurosurgeon on the staff is ready for him," Dr. Thomas said. "The decision to proceed is based on consultation."

"His chances?"

The doctor shrugged. "No chance if we don't move quickly."

"I want to be in the operating room," Hogan said.

"There's an observation theater adjoining the operating room."

"Not good enough," Hogan said. "You can sterilize me or whatever you have to do, but I'm going to be right there with him."

"That's highly irregular, Sergeant."

"Murder is highly irregular," Hogan said.

It was a little after four in the afternoon when Dan Garvey was wheeled into the operating room. Quist, behind glass that separated the observation theater from the operating room, watched what seemed to be an endless procedure. The surgeon was assisted by Dr. Thomas, two other doctors, and a corps of surgical nurses. Standing to one side, gowned and masked, was Sergeant Hogan. A handful of nurses and interns and a constantly changing number of doctors circulated in the theater around Quist.

It went on, hour after hour. Quist had no idea what he was seeing, but as long as the surgeon kept working it meant that Dan was alive. It was going on eleven o'clock at night when the surgeon moved away from the table, this time with an air of finality. Every bone in Quist's body ached as he made his way into the hallway beyond the theater. Dr. Thomas, looking exhausted, came out a side door.

"A magnificent job," he said.

"He's going to make it?"

"My dear Mr. Quist, it's far too soon to answer that

question with any certainty. Dr. Metzger did everything, surgically, that could be done. I won't go technical because you wouldn't know what I was talking about. But the injury was inflicted on your friend a good many hours ago—perhaps as much as a day ago. If we'd had him at once, his chances would be better. He was terribly weakened by the long delay. We can hope. That's the best I can give you."

"Will he be able to talk?"

"Not for days, I'd guess. If he survives for days. God, man, they beat the hell out of your friend."

Dan, unless he was caught completely off guard, must have put up some kind of fight of his own. Someone, somewhere would show the marks of that fight.

"Can you make any kind of a guess about the weapon used? You don't fracture a skull with a fist."

Dr. Thomas shrugged. "Gun butt, tire iron, metal wrecking bar."

"Bastards!" Quist said.

Quist was bone tired, spent from the long vigil outside the operating room, but a fierce anger kept him moving. He decided to touch base with Lydia and Rosemary Wilson, self-imprisoned in his apartment, and then head back for the Complex. Time was working for a killer, or killers; time could be used to cover clues, to take off to the ends of the earth, out of reach forever.

He parked his Mercedes in front of the apartment building on Beekman Place and told George, the night doorman, that he'd only be a few minutes.

Lydia's arms around him, her cheek pressed against his, acted as a reviver. Rosie Wilson, Ed Smythe's kid, stood a distance away, wide-eyed, waiting for news. Quist, still holding Lydia, described his day, the word from Kreevich about Dan, the ordeal at the hospital.

"If it is to be days before Dan can talk, what happens next?" Lydia asked, knowing the answer before he gave it.

"I'm going back out to the Complex," Quist said. "Among other things, I've walked out on Willie Jacobs. He can be in the same kind of trouble as Dan."

"Isn't that now up to Mark Kreevich and the police out at the Complex?" Lydia asked.

"Police move like turtles," Quist said. "Slow and solid."

"Not Mark."

"Even Mark," Quist said. "They have to go by the book."

"But what can you do that they can't do?" Lydia asked. "You're in the same danger Dan was in, Julian. They know you and what you're looking for, but you don't know who they are."

"Some sonofabitch out there has all the answers," Quist said. "If I can find him, I won't have to wait for a warrant, or an assistant district attorney to ask him questions. I can beat it out of him, and I will if I find him."

PART THREE

1

There were times, Lydia thought, when Julian and Dan Garvey became almost interchangeable. Dan, dashing off impulsively to fight the whole world, would have been given calm and rational advice by Julian—and ignored it. Julian, in the grip of a rage at what had happened to people he cared for, could be just as impulsive as Dan, just as immune to common-sense counseling. It was absurd, Lydia told herself, for him to embark on a one-man crusade against "they." But nothing on earth would stop him except his own common sense, if it ever surfaced.

She could stall for time, hoping he would see it another way. She poured him a double Jack Daniels on the rocks. While he sat at the little chromium-trimmed bar, sipping it, she went into the adjoining kitchenette to make him a sandwich, knowing he'd probably eaten nothing since breakfast.

"Ambrosia!" he said, when he tasted the ham-and-cheese sandwich flavored with hot Dijon mustard.

But he would go, she knew.

All the time this was going on, Rosemary Wilson had sat

huddled in a corner of the couch, listening intently to what Quist had to say as though her life depended upon it. Perhaps, Lydia thought, it did.

"I guess I'm not supposed to have an opinion about anything, am I?" Rosemary finally said, in a small voice. "You know, Julian, you're talking about a world I know better than you do."

Quist turned to look at the intense, eager young face.

"There are all kinds of worlds out there at the Complex," Rosie said, "and you only know one of them."

"Go ahead, Rosie. What's on your mind?"

"You only know the rich people, the important people, the Jerry Carpenters, the Young Millionaires Ed was always talking about. They pay you to sell what they own, right?"

"They pay me to sell sports, entertainment."

"So they sit high up somewhere and count the gate receipts, and figure their tax deductions, and take the credit for everything, right? But there are a whole lot of different worlds with different interests, Julian. There's a whole army of people who mow the lawns and tend the flower beds and pick up the candy wrappers and empty cigarette packages people throw around. That's one army that works outside, mostly when the crowds aren't there. Then there's another army that keeps the Arena building clean, changes the Arena itself from an ice-skating rink to a basketball court to a tanbark surface for horse shows, checks the light bulbs and the heating system and the air-conditioning. That's the maintenance army. Then there are the athletes who play the games, and their managers and agents, and their own private promotional people, and the people who run the leagues they play in. That's the world of performers, right? Then there's the world I really know—the people who care for and work with horses: the grooms, the stable hands, the jockeys, the exercise boys—and girls like me—the horse doctors, the blacksmiths, the track stewards, the crew that works the starting gates, grounds keepers who scrape and grade the track, and everyone else whose job it is to see to it that the horses run well and honestly." She laughed, nervously.

"Someone in that army missed the boat on King Lear," Quist said.

"Maybe, maybe not," Rosie said. "There is still another army, Julian. They are the touts, the con men, the cheap crooks who pick your pockets, the fix artists who are always trying to set up a sure thing and manage it now and then, I guess. Not only horse races, but fights and team games."

"And the thousands of people who come every day to watch the games, the shows, the fights, the races," Quist said.

"They pay their way in," Rosie said. "They are the potential suckers."

"And the point of all this, Rosie?" Quist asked.

"It's Ed Smythe's world, his army, that is behind what's happened to your friend Dan, and maybe to Willie Jacobs," she said. "You don't think it was one of your millionaire friends who slugged Dan Garvey, hid him under a tarpaulin on a pickup truck, and abandoned him in the city, do you? That was someone from my world, Julian. Someone who murdered Mrs. Cameron and tried to cover it by torturing a horse. Someone who drove poor Ed to kill himself."

"Someone who may be dealing in millions of dollars in drugs," Quist said.

"There will be whispers in the world I know, Julian, whispers you'll never hear. My people will clam up at the sight of you, or of a cop or a security man. But in their special places—in a tack room, huddled around a fire and a coffeepot off Shed Row—they will talk. Some of them will talk to me because I was Ed Smythe's kid, and Ed was liked and respected. They'll talk in the night, in the dark, in the quiet hours when they'll feel safe, hidden. I've got to go back there, Julian. I can't stay locked up here any longer."

"With someone waiting for you," Lydia said. "Ready to make sure you don't pass on what they think Ed Smythe may have told you!"

"I wonder," Quist said, looking thoughtfully at Rosie.

"You wonder!" Lydia sounded outraged. "You're the one who's had us locked up here for twenty-four hours, not answering the phone. You wonder?"

"The climate changes with time," Quist said. "It's almost twenty-four hours since Rosie came here, followed by young Teliski and Grogan. Rosie was a danger to them—Ed Smythe may have told her something. But a whole day has gone by and nothing has happened. If Rosie knew something and told it to me, why haven't I passed it on to the police? And why haven't the police acted on that information? Because Rosie didn't have anything to tell. So she's no longer a threat to them, and I'm no longer a threat, and you, my love, are no longer a threat."

"So we're off the hook," Lydia said. "Let's stay off it!" She knew what he was thinking. She was way ahead of him.

"Rosie's right, you know," he said. "There are things to be heard out there at the Complex, whispers in the dark. One way or another I mean to hear them—for Dan, for Judith, for Willie, and for us. I can't let them run out on us, Lydia. All traces of the truth can disappear, given time."

"You're going to walk out on Dan?" Lydia asked, trying a last ploy.

"I can't help Dan there in the hospital," Quist said. "The only thing I can do for him is finish the job he set out to do.

There is someone at the Complex about to get away with murder. It mustn't happen, love."

"They stopped Dan, they can stop you," Lydia said.

"They can try," Quist said.

Be sure to dress for it, Kreevich had said. "Be sure to dress for someone taking a shot at you from behind a tree, or a barn, or the next booth in the men's room." The Homicide man hadn't been kidding.

Quist's whole life style operated on the theory that it paid to be noticed. His mod wardrobe, the beautiful lady always on his arm, a kind of public flamboyance, was part of a conscious attempt to attract attention. It was good for business. It was good for business for him and Lydia to be seen at glamour parties, at the discos, the night places. It was good for business to be mentioned by Liz Smith and the other columnists who covered another world, the world of the "beautiful people."

Tonight was different. Quist took time to change into a dark blue tropical worsted suit, a black knit sports shirt, black shoes. Tonight it would be wiser to fade into the shadows of Rosie Wilson's world, the world of shots from behind a tree, or a barn, or, as in Dan Garvey's case, a clobbering from behind with an iron bar. From the handkerchief drawer of his bureau he took a small, flat handgun that long ago he had been licensed to carry. Tonight the unexpected would be expected.

"Bad as that?"

He turned to find Lydia standing in the doorway to his dressing room. She was staring at the little gun that rested in the palm of his hand. He shrugged, and slipped the gun into the side pocket of his dark blue suit coat. He crossed over to her and stood with his hands on her shoulders.

"It's really just a stage prop," he said. "Might give me some leverage if someone gets too stubborn."

She looked up at him. "I think I'm entitled to an honest answer to one question, Julian."

"You have it," he said. He bent down and brushed her forehead with his lips.

"Why is it important for you to involve yourself in this?" she asked. "There are the State Police and Captain Mowery, there are Victor Lorch and his security people, there is Mark Kreevich. All professionals. I know how good you are at this sort of thing, Julian, but if Mark is right, you're up against a gang, a mob, an army. That stage prop in your pocket isn't much to use against them."

"Don't worry," he said, sounding very casual. "If it comes to a shootout I'll leave it to your pros."

"Will they give you that choice, Julian? Did they give Dan that choice? Or Judith?"

He had to give it to her straight. "I drove Dan into this by convincing him that Judith had been murdered, not killed by a horse. I dragged Willie Jacobs into it by asking, openly, for his help."

"So your conscience bothers you," Lydia said. "Does that equip you to confront an unidentified gang of killers?"

"Rosie's right, you know," he said. "We're dealing with a lot of interlocking worlds out there. They all have one thing in common. They don't like cops, they don't trust cops. They won't talk to cops."

"Surely they know how close you are to Lorch, to Mark. Doesn't that make you an ally of cops?"

Quist's face hardened. "My closest friend may or may not make it," he said. "His lady is dead, cut to pieces by the medical examiner's autopsy. I have a personal stake in this, love, with which people in Rosie's worlds may sympathize. There is a chance that Rosie and I may get to hear things that the cops never would. Just one whisper of truth, just one informed speculation, might break this wide open. I can't back away from that chance, Lydia."

"Tomorrow, after you've gotten some rest—?"

"Tomorrow may be too late. Whatever it is they're trying to hide, whatever it is they'll kill for to hide, may be permanently hidden by tomorrow."

She stared at him for a moment, then lowered her face and rested it against his shoulder. "You have to do what you have to do," she said. Then she looked up again. "I'm not going to stay here alone, Julian, waiting and waiting to hear something!"

"I suggest you go to the hospital and stay with Dan," Quist said. "Mark has a man there guarding him. I don't want you anywhere alone, because 'they' might try to use you to turn me off. Mark's man can protect you, and how wonderful it would be for Dan if he should come out of it and you were there."

"I'm thinking how wonderful it would be if I come out of it and you are here," she said.

He took her in his arms and held her very close. "Just remember, my darling, that we live charmed lives," he said softly.

It was after one o'clock in the morning when Quist wheeled his Mercedes into the parking lot at the Complex. Lydia, with no further protests, had been dropped off at St. Vincent's to be with Dan. Kreevich had given assurance that Sergeant Hogan or his relief man would be instructed to keep a special eye on Lydia.

"What I ought to do is place you in protective custody," Kreevich had said on the phone.

"I don't make sense?" Quist had asked.

"It makes sense of a sort," Kreevich had said. "But it's

your neck, your life. I'm letting Lorch know you're on your way out there."

"That would seem to make me safe as a church."

"We can hope."

Rosie Wilson, huddled down in the passenger seat beside Quist, rode almost the whole distance from the city to the Complex without speaking a word. About a hundred yards from the entrance gates to the Complex, Quist stopped the car and let her out. It had been agreed they shouldn't be seen together for now. She would slip quietly into her world to listen to whatever there was to hear. Their point of contact would be Lorch's office in the Arena Building. The people who seemed to connect with the violence were Ben Diamond, the young Teliski, and Pat Grogan. Where were they? What were they up to? The people around Shed Row must be asking themselves those questions.

The girl looked terribly small, almost helpless, as she stood outside the car looking at Quist. A child! For a moment he felt like calling her back, telling her to forget the whole thing. Yet her presence in Shed Row would seem perfectly normal to the night workers there. She belonged. She had the best opportunity of anyone to come up with something useful.

There should have been a moon, but the night was overcast, clouded over, the threat of a summer shower in the air. Looking in his rear-view mirror as he drove on, Quist saw Rosie swallowed up in the darkness.

Inside the grounds the Stirrup Cup was a blaze of lights. The collection of cars parked outside suggested they were doing a thriving business. Quist knew that the bar stayed open till three o'clock. Even though it had been a dark night at the Arena—no scheduled event—the Stirrup Cup attracted people with its fine food, its incomparable wine cellar, and the certainty that friends would be congregated there.

Business didn't seem to be affected by whether or not there was some sporting event scheduled, only that more people were turned away on an event night.

Like many other ventures at the Complex, Julian Quist Associates had been involved in finding the right man to manage the Stirrup Cup. He was Michael Romano, stolen away from New York's Hotel Beaumont, top luxury hotel. Mike Romano knew restaurant management, knew the art of perfect service, and knew how to handle the very rich and demanding clientele the Stirrup Cup attracted.

Romano, a dark, handsome Italian wearing a custom-tailored dinner jacket, spotted Quist almost the moment he came through the front entrance into the lobby. There the hopeful looked past a red velvet rope that shut them off from the main room until the maître d' could find a place for them. Quist let Romano steer him into the manager's private office. Rosie Wilson might hear the whispers in the stable area, but if there was any talk in the glamour department, Mike Romano would have heard it.

"We know the news about Dan out here," Romano said. "How is it with him?"

"Not good," Quist said. "He has a chance—that's the best they'll say."

"My God," Romano said. "He's the last man in the world to get caught off guard by some thug. What do the police say? I pour you a Jack Daniels as usual?"

"This is a night to stay sober," Quist said. "A little Perrier water and a slice of lime, if you have it."

Romano's office was like a pleasant living room in a country house: early American furniture, handsome chintz curtains pulled across the windows, early Currier and Ives horse-racing prints on the walls. Opening off one end of it was a kitchenette, and off the other a conventional office with filing cabinets and office machinery. The main room was where Romano received customers with complaints or credit problems.

"It wasn't just any thug, you know, Mike," Quist said, when the manager had brought his drink back from the kitchenette. "It had to be someone connected with Judith Cameron's death. Ben Diamond is the cops' number-one choice. He was seen driving a pickup truck earlier in the day. Dan was dumped into such a truck, under a tarpaulin, and left to die. Driven into the city."

"You think it happened out here?"

Romano sat behind his flat-topped desk, going through the ritual of lighting a cigarette. His dark eyes were bright with a kind of anger. Dan was his friend. Dan had so many friends.

"Where else?" Quist said. "Dan's car is still parked out on Shed Row where he left it day before yesterday. He was looking for a killer, but it seems the killer found him."

"Talk. There is nothing but talk since Mrs. Cameron was found dead," Romano said. "Mostly talk about a ringer horse."

"You buy it?" Quist asked.

Romano shrugged. A pale cloud of cigarette smoke drifted away, attracted by the air-conditioning exhaust. "People say Ed Smythe's suicide clinches it. People say he knew he was going to be caught out. The police say he killed Mrs. Cameron and then couldn't take it."

"Just between us, Mike," Quist said. "Before Smythe died he talked about a sellout, a piece of forty-seven million dollars. That's out of the league of a ringer horse that might have made someone a few thousand bucks. Lieutenant Kreevich is thinking drugs, with South America as a source and Smythe a recent visitor there."

"I hadn't heard that Smythe talked before he died,"

Romano said. "The story I heard was that he was dead when you and Willie Jacobs found him."

"He talked," Quist said. He had no intention of involving Rosie Wilson, even though he trusted Romano.

"Drugs!" Romano brought his fist down on the desk in front of him. "You know something, Julian? My grandfather was a bootlegger—selling illegal liquor. He never thought he was doing anybody any harm because he sold good stuff. Nobody ever got sick or went blind or anything from drinking the liquor the old man sold. Oh, I know there are people who think any liquor is a poison. But drugs! That stuff is poisoning the world today, and it's everywhere. Kids start it in grade school, for God sake. I come on it every day here at the Cup. My kitchen help, my waiters. You walk around out there in the main room where the rich customers are, look into their faces. If you know the signs—the enlarged pupils, the little beads of sweat on a forehead or an upper lip, the twitching of a nerve—you'll see it. Half the people out there. The rich can afford it and they go for it. The poor can't afford it and they mug, steal, and kill for it. I hate it! The dealers, the sellers, have no compassion for the addict. The poor bastard has to have it, and if he can't afford it, let him go off his rocker. If what happened to Mrs. Cameron, to Dan, to Ed Smythe has to do with dealers in drugs, I'll go to the wall with you to get the sonsofbitches!"

"What wall?" Quist asked.

"Right here is the wall," Romano said. "A place where thousands of people come and go every day. In a crowd can you tell a dealer from anyone else? He looks like anyone else—like a hockey fan, a fight fan, a horse lover. The buyer passes him in the crowd and a package, smaller than a pack of cigarettes, changes hands. Forty-seven million dollars, you said? You think that's truckloads of stuff? The Coast

Guard picked up a boat the other day with forty million dollars worth of coke—street value—hidden in a few dozen automobile tires! The Complex is a heaven for buyers and sellers of poison. Sure, I'll go to the wall with you, Julian, but it's ten-to-one we come up empty."

"Why? Why such long odds?"

"Fear," Romano said. "The drug traffic isn't in the hands of small-fry. It's a big, international business. You talk about South America? I've been told there are over five hundred small airports that are shipping points for the stuff. They have small planes flying all the time from out-of-the-way places down there to out-of-the-way places up here. How to stop it? It's like catching flies in a fishnet. A kilo of heroin is worth about two hundred thousand dollars on the street. You know how much that is in size and weight, Julian? A kilo is 2.2 pounds—like two pounds of butter with a couple of pats left over. You mentioned forty-odd million dollars Ed Smythe talked about?"

"Yes."

"You can add it up on your fingers," Romano said. "A kilo 2.2 pounds in bulk is worth two hundred thousand. A hundred kilos is worth twenty million. Two hundred kilos is worth forty million. But you don't need the United States Navy to bring it in, Julian. We're talking about maybe five hundred pounds of powder—the size of two good defensive tackles on the Dallas Cowboys football team! Flown in, in small amounts from hundreds of different places to hundreds of different places, and you're talking about stuff that can be brought in hip-pocket amounts by hundreds of different carriers. Or if they want to bring in a big load all in one piece it's possible, like I said, in a few automobile tires on some freighter carrying a Greek flag. Our government gets lucky if they can intercept a tiny fraction of what comes in. Less than three pounds, worth a quarter of a million, can be hidden in the lining of a suitcase, in a woman's girdle for God sake, sewn into an overcoat. That's how easy it is, and how almost impossible it is for the government to block it out. In my grandfather's day one quart of booze was hard to carry unnoticed. In the drug traffic you can carry a small fortune inside your hatband!"

"You started to talk about fear?" Quist said.

"Oh brother, is there fear!" Romano ground out his cigarette in the ashtray on his desk. "The big boys who own the traffic don't fool around with their carriers, their distributors, their street-corner and back-door peddlers. They'd be out of business in five minutes if anybody ever got away with anything. It's like computerized. X has so much to get rid of. He must return an exact amount. If he stops on the way home and drops a few hundred bucks in a dice game, he's got to make it up when he pays in. Or goodbye Mr. X. There's only one penalty in that business, Julian. Mr. X isn't just reprimanded. He winds up with a bullet in his head, buried in someone's back yard in Westchester or New Jersey. No excuses are acceptable. They play it that way because if they didn't they'd be stolen blind."

"Why run the risk?"

"Because your own drug needs will be supplied for as long as you keep your nose clean. When you've got the habit, you'll run any risk to feed it. But fear is with them from the time they get up in the morning to the time they fall into bed at night. The fear of dying, which is the worst fear of all, Julian."

"No reprieve from any kind of failure?"

Romano's laugh was short and sharp. "You're carrying a couple of kilos sewed into your suitcase. You're flying from some little airport in Peru to, say, Jackson, Mississippi. Your plane crashes and burns, but you're lucky enough to walk away from it. Your suitcase with the coke in it burns up in the plane. Goodbye Mr. X! It may appear to be an act of God, but the Big Boys won't risk the chance that you walked away with a fortune. Dead men never get to enjoy the profits from a double cross, or even a remotely possible double cross."

"So if Ed Smythe's 'sellout' had to do with drugs, and he crossed the Big Boys in some fashion, then he would know his number was up and he beat them to it?"

"If he crossed them, his number would certainly have been up," Romano said.

"You think Dan may have stumbled across the drug scene in some way?" Quist asked.

"One thing makes me question it," Romano said, after a moment's hesitation. "He's still alive. The Big Boys aren't usually that careless."

Romano's name for them was "the Big Boys." Ed Smythe had simply called them "they."

"According to the doctor," Quist said, "whoever slugged Dan had every reason to think he'd totaled him. Tell me, Mike, where do I start to look for these 'Big Boys,' the guys at the top?"

Romano spread his hands. "Who knows? Maybe some of them are sitting out there in the restaurant right now. For a number of years now, Julian, I've asked questions of quite a few poor slobs who came my way, caught up in the habit. I never got a name from anyone. I never heard a name mentioned by the cops. Your man Vic Lorch has been trying to keep if off the Complex lot. He's come up with a few small-time peddlers, but there's never been a big name. He'll tell you. I guess you stay anonymous at the top or you join your late associate in those Westchester and Jersey gardens."

"Tell me about Jerry Carpenter," Quist said.

"Jerry?" Romano looked surprised. "One of my best

customers. He's out front with a party now. Five- or six-hundred-dollar tab before the night's over."

"It's curious how it all revolves around him, and yet no one thinks he can be involved."

"Revolves around him?" Romano asked.

"It starts with his horse winning a race it shouldn't have won," Quist said. "If it wasn't his horse, it at least ran out of his stable. Mrs. Cameron was killed in that horse's stall in his stable area, either by his horse or by Ben Diamond, his stable hand who was, he says, trying to rescue the lady. Or by Ed Smythe, his man. Dan, by the way, was found in a pickup truck like one Diamond, Carpenter's man, was seen driving earlier in the day. Ed Smythe, Carpenter's head groom, commits suicide after talking about millions of dollars and a sellout. There isn't a single aspect of this whole thing that doesn't touch Carpenter somewhere. What about him, Mike? I've had drinks with him, chatted casually here and there, but I don't really know him."

Romano gestured toward Quist's drink.

"Thanks, no," Quist said. "It doesn't really do anything for me. When I come up with something, I'll drink you dry. About Carpenter?"

"He's almost unreal," Romano said, lighting a fresh cigarette. "I don't think in his whole life he's had a single day when he faced any serious responsibility. A lot of young men expect to inherit, and wait around for it, and amount to nothing while they're waiting. Jerry's mother died when he was about fifteen years old and left him so much it boggles the mind. His father died when he was in college and left him another chunk. This boy could lend money to the Government for the national debt. There is no reason in God's world for him ever to get involved in anything crooked—for money, that is."

"For some other reason?"

"I'm not a psychiatrist," Romano said, his eyes narrowed against the smoke from his cigarette.

"Take a crack at it."

"When you don't have to lift a finger to get anything in the world you want," Romano said slowly, "you must ask yourself questions. Could I lift a finger if I had to? You must know that people look at you as an ineffectual playboy. Damaging to the ego, wouldn't you say? So some big shot comes along and says, 'How would you like to take a risk on something?' It wouldn't be an investment. He doesn't need money. But suppose he was asked to risk his freedom, risk going to jail, perhaps even risk his life? Would he think that would make him look like a big shot to people who think he's a nothing? He might need to look daring, like a hot shot to someone, anyone." Romano leaned forward. "You know, when I first heard this talk—yesterday, was it?—about a ringer, I actually thought it could be that Jerry was behind it. Not to make money betting at long odds, you understand, but to be able to say to Mrs. Cameron that he'd been *right* all along about the horse."

"And when she found out, killed her?"

"No," Romano said. "No, no, no. He'd have admitted he'd pulled a fast one, as a joke on the lady. He'd have paid off anyone who'd lost money by it. Even that would have done something for his ego. But kill her? Torture a horse? Never. It's just not in his cards, Julian."

"Poor little rich boy," Quist said, and stood up. "The night's going by me, Mike."

"I told you Jerry's out front with a party," Romano said. "He'll be anxious to know how Dan is doing. He asked me several times, earlier in the evening, if I'd heard anything."

The horse is, of course, the keynote of the Stirrup Cup's decor. There are paintings of famous thoroughbreds, glassed-in cabinets containing trophies and other memorabilia of racing history. The bartenders wear replicas of racing silks. It is not a dark room. The fluorescent lighting is cunningly designed so that while the room is bright there is no glare from anywhere. This is not a place to hide but to be seen.

Jerry Carpenter and his party, at a large circular table in the center of the room, were very visible. There were two other male members of the party who were known to Quist: Juan Ricardo, the South American sportsman, and Matthew Boylan, the chairman of the Complex's board of directors. There were two other men, strangers to Quist, and five rather garish-looking girls, none of whom Quist remembered seeing before.

Carpenter spotted Quist as he came into the room, rose from the table, and came directly to where Quist and Romano stood together.

"News of Dan?" Carpenter asked, genuinely concerned.

"Hanging in," Quist said. "It's still pretty iffy."

"How ghastly," Carpenter said. "Is there anything at all anyone can do?"

"Pray, if it fits your scheme of things," Quist said.

"Won't you join us for a drink?" Carpenter asked. "We've all been talking about Dan, worrying about him, wondering what happened to him."

"We don't know what happened to him," Quist said. "Someone tried to beat out his brains, dumped him in a truck, left him for dead. Where, when, who—we don't know. Nor why."

They had reached the table. Ricardo greeted Quist with his white smile. Boylan gave him a curt nod. The names of the other men and the women meant nothing—except for one. The bosomy blonde sitting next to Boylan was Claire Kingman, the lady of the evening who lived around the corner from Quist's Beekman Place apartment. His attention focused on her. Quist thought he recognized the signs Romano had mentioned to him: the pupils of her dark blue eyes were dilated, a thin film of perspiration dotted her upper lip. On the stuff, he thought. She seemed aware of his special attention and gave him a bright, theatrical smile.

"I understand I came into your life last night, Mr. Quist," she said. "Two young goons from out here, hanging around my place. I understand you were called on to vouch for them."

"Couldn't. I don't know either of them," Quist said.

"And won't get to," Boylan said. A big, aged-speckled hand covered the girl's. "I had them both kicked off the lot today. Wise-guy jerks!"

"You've told Jerry about your friend Garvey?" Ricardo asked.

Quist repeated the report. "I was wondering if you or Jerry knew anything about Ben Diamond. He was seen yesterday driving a truck that could be the one in which Dan was found."

"You think I would know about him?" Ricardo asked. "I know him, of course. He was with Jerry's horses in Argentina this past season. I knew him and the unfortunate Smythe there. I kept an eye on Jerry's interests there. But this Diamond and I were not what you might call—chums!"

"He just evaporated after the police turned him loose," Carpenter said.

"I mentioned that he was seen driving a pickup truck yesterday morning. He stopped at the house where he boarded, paid up his landlord, took his things, and drove off. Something under a tarpaulin in the back of the truck. Connecticut license plates—the witness thinks."

"Can't the police trace the registration?" Ricardo asked.

"When the police found the pickup, with Dan stashed away under the tarpaulin, the license plates were missing."

"If it's the same truck," Ricardo said.

Quist gave the dark, smiling man a hard look. "If it's the same truck," he said. "You have to swallow a lot of coincidence to suppose it isn't, Mr. Ricardo."

"Your witness can't tell you the plate numbers?"

"An old man. He had no reason to remember the numbers. But he noticed the plates were blue and white—Connecticut."

"Why abandon the truck on a city street where it was certain to be examined—with Dan in it?" Carpenter asked. "And remove the plates?"

"Removing the plates is obvious," Quist said. "We don't know who owns the truck. Perhaps they wanted it found, with what they thought was a dead man under the tarpaulin. A warning to anyone who was trying to find what Dan was trying to find."

"Judith's killer," Carpenter said.

"If that's what Dan was trying to find," Quist said.

"What else?" Ricardo asked.

Quist looked around at the ten people who were focused intently on him. This was not the place to mention what he suspected. Any one of these people could be connected with what Romano had called "the Big Boys." He led them down another street.

"If King Lear was not King Lear," he said. "If that's what Judith Cameron discovered and why she was killed, then Dan may have found himself on the same trail."

"You don't know when Garvey was attacked," Matt Boylan said, speaking for the first time. "Most of a day went by before you found Smythe with a hose in his mouth. There was time for him to polish off Garvey as well as Mrs. Cameron, drive the body into the city, come back to his house and do himself in. Time for him to think, while he was driving back and forth, that he was up the creek—no way he wouldn't be caught. Why do you keep shying away from Smythe, Quist? It's so obvious. He'd have access to any truck that was parked around Shed Row. If the horse was a ringer, he had to be in on it, he and Diamond. He got in over his head, tried to save himself, and finally saw it was hopeless."

Quist gave the chairman a steady look. "A friend of mine on Manhattan Homicide has an axiom he believes in, Mr. Boylan. The man who pulls the trigger is not necessarily the killer we want. We want the man who hires him to do it. You could be right about Smythe. But the person I'm interested in, if you *are* right, is the man who persuaded him to risk the job he loved, the safety of a daughter he loved, his life itself. The bait that persuaded him to risk his whole world must have been enormous. I'm interested in the man who made him the offer. The Law may be satisfied that it has a murderer, but true justice won't be satisfied until we have the man who planned it and corrupted someone to carry it out."

2

From the steps leading up to Vic Lorch's office in the Arena Building, Quist had a clear view of the Shed Row area. There were very few artificial lights. Hundreds of horses were kept quiet and in the dark for necessary rest. There was not the bustle and scurry that kept the place so busy in daylight hours. On the outskirts Quist saw three or four open fires, and he knew that stable hands and watchmen sat around them, drinking coffee, absorbed in the endless topics of the world of the horse. Tonight, Quist thought, there would be talk of murder, and suicide, and the possibility that a ringer horse had won a race. Rosie Wilson could be sitting at one of those fires, listening, hopefully hearing something that would help.

Lorch was in his office.

"Kreevich told me you were on your way out here," he told Quist. "Coffee?"

"Thanks." Quist sat down in a folding canvas armchair, aware, suddenly, of his physical fatigue. They talked briefly about Dan, his condition, his prospects. Lorch, who counted Dan as his friend, was grim.

"So help me God," he said, "if I can lay hands on the person or people responsible, the cops won't have to bother with questions. I'll have torn the answers out of them!"

The same thing Quist had said to Lydia.

" 'Them,' " Quist said. "We never have names to put to them. All we have are the foot soldiers: Ed Smythe who's dead; Ben Diamond who's disappeared; young Teliski and Grogan who have, I understand, been fired by the management. None of them have the brains or resources to handle a multimillion-dollar drug deal."

"If that's what it is," Lorch said.

"You have a better guess, Vic?"

"No. Incidentally, there's been another firing. Carpenter dropped Bull Teliski, his night watchman who is Pete Teliski's old man."

"He didn't mention that to me when I saw him just now," Quist said. "Why did he fire the man?" A thought ran through his mind. Bull Teliski had been absent from his post, legitimately it had seemed, when Judith Cameron had been killed. Covering for another watchman, he'd said.

"Bull Teliski is a character," Lorch said. "Some other time you'd enjoy him. He's an ex-prizefighter. He's got a story about every fighter you ever heard of. He fought a lot of the best ones and got beat by most of them. He looks like a battlefield: bent and flattened nose, thick upper lip, scar tissue around his eyes, a cauliflower ear. But he's so honest it hurts. Except yesterday."

"And yesterday?"

"He lied about giving his kid and young Grogan permission to use Carpenter's stable car to drive to the city. He covered for Pete, his son, when the boy gave that explanation to Kreevich. But he couldn't live with it. He didn't mind lying to the cops—that's his way of life. But he couldn't stand lying to the man he worked for, Jerry Carpenter.

Carpenter laughed it off when Bull told him, said he understood how Bull would cover up for his boy. But a few hours later he showed up in Shed Row and gave Bull the gate. I have to think Matt Boylan was behind it. He was steamed up over young Pete and Grogan nosing around after the Kingman doll. He fired them early in the day. He must have put the heat on Jerry Carpenter to get rid of the Bull."

"The lady's over in the Stirrup Cup now with Boylan," Quist said. "Unless I'm very much mistaken, she's stoned to the gills on some kind of dope."

"It's a way of life for a hell of a lot of people I have to say 'Sir' to," Lorch said.

"If that kind of people weren't the customers, there might not be a billion-dollar traffic."

"I wish that was true," Lorch said. "Mat Boylan can afford to supply his tootsie with whatever she wants. If she wants to rot out her brains and he wants to help her do it, I don't give a damn. It's the school kids, the street kids, the people who are hooked and have to steal to get it, that bother me. They find the money for it, no matter where and how, and the mob makes a fortune out of that kind of violence. We pick up a pusher or two every time there's an event out here, but it never leads to anyone who matters."

"No one ever talks?"

"Most of them are on the stuff themselves. If they talk, the supply is cut off."

"Or, if Mike Romano is right, they wind up buried in someone's flower garden."

"That's the scenario we hear," Lorch said.

"So where do we look for Ben Diamond?" Quist asked.

Lorch shrugged. "No one's seen him since yesterday. Your old man at the boardinghouse is the last one to see him that we've heard of. My men have been over this place from one end to the other. No word or sign of him."

"He could know everything we need to know," Quist said.

"I doubt it," Lorch said. "You want the people at the top. For sure a manure pusher like Diamond doesn't know who they are. Somebody one step above him gave him his orders, paid him his money. That's a long way from what you're shooting at, friend. If we find him you won't be any closer. He can't tell you what he doesn't know."

"So where, goddamnit, do we go?" Quist asked, his anger spilling over.

"Maybe you just came from the right place," Lorch said.

"The Stirrup Cup?"

"Where the big money moves around," Lorch said.

"You just sit around while they laugh at you?" Quist said. "You don't have a wedge to pry anything loose."

"That's been the name of the game for years," Lorch said. "It's the biggest business in the world, next to oil."

"Dan must have been close, or why work him over?"

"But close to what?" Lorch said. "Like fitting one piece into a giant jigsaw puzzle. That's as far as they'll let you go."

"But what Dan found was here, here on the grounds of the Complex," Quist said.

"Be my guest," Lorch said.

They were two angry, frustrated men.

There was a sharp knock at the door of the office. Lorch shouted an invitation to come in. A young man entered wearing blue jeans, a pale blue workshirt, a dark cap pulled down over a suntanned face. He hesitated when he saw Quist.

"It's okay, Terry," Lorch said. "This is Terry Davis—Julian Quist. Terry's one of my boys, Julian, working under cover on Shed Row."

"I know who Mr. Quist is," Davis said. "Is there any news on Dan Garvey, Mr. Quist? Everybody's asking."

"Touch and go," Quist said.

"The cops know what happened?" Davis asked.

"Just that somebody damn near beat his brains out," Quist said. "Left him for dead in the back of a pickup truck."

"You didn't come here to ask about Dan, Terry," Lorch said.

Davis nodded. He was surprisingly young looking, Quist thought, to be part of the security team. He hadn't known that Lorch had people working under cover. Davis looked more like an exercise boy than a cop.

"There's some kind of a rumble cooking down on Shed Row," Davis said. "It centers around the Carpenter horses. You know how things are there, Vic—Smythe dead, Diamond gone somewhere, Bull Teliski fired in the afternoon by Carpenter. Regulars all cleaned out. Carpenter's brought in five guys to take over."

"Five guys?" Lorch said. "An army, for Christ sake!"

"Pretty tough-looking guys who don't look as though they know which end of the horse eats," Davis said.

Lorch looked at Quist. "One watchman, Bull Teliski, is all they ever had before."

"These strong-arm boys have blocked off the alleys," Davis said. "People who want to get to other stables have to walk around to the far end to get in. The regulars don't like it. They don't like strangers around at night. They don't like being policed. It looks like somebody might start something."

"Carpenter didn't have any choice but to bring in strangers," Lorch said.

"Five of them to guard nine horses?" Davis asked. "Five guys with guns?"

"Guns?"

"I know the bulge of a shoulder holster when I see it," Davis said. "Some of the regulars are going to decide to walk their usual routes, and that's going to start trouble."

Lorch stood up. "Somebody's got to be talked out of something," he said. "If Carpenter's still down at the Stirrup Cup, maybe he can explain what his boys are up to. What about Hank Benson, the trainer? He'd be in charge, wouldn't he?"

"Nobody's seen him all night," Davis said. "These five guys just walked in and took over."

"Let's find Carpenter," Lorch said. "Get back to the Row and keep your ears open, Terry. Do what you can to talk the regulars out of starting anything."

Quist stopped the undercover man as he started to leave. "Have you seen Ed Smythe's girl down there?" He asked.

Davis looked surprised. "Rose? She wouldn't be around this time of night."

"She's somewhere down there," Quist said.

"I've been circulating all night," Davis said. "Haven't seen her."

What Jerry Carpenter did about new night watchmen, and how the regulars on Shed Row reacted to it, was not Quist's primary concern at that moment. It had started two days ago with Judith Cameron, a friend; then Dan and Willie Jacobs, both friends, had vanished for a day. Dan was unhappily accounted for, but not Willie. Now Rosie Wilson wasn't where she was supposed to be. Quist had let himself be talked into sending her off on her own, and he felt responsible.

Terry Davis, the undercover security man, had a special way of coming and going to and from Lorch's office without attracting attention.

"Word got around I have any connection with Vic and I'd stop being useful," he told Quist. His route led down through the Arena basement, through the utility rooms, and out a fire door on the opposite side of the huge building. He didn't want Quist to go with him. "I don't want to be seen with you, either, Mr. Quist. Speak to me down at Shed Row, like you might speak to anyone you don't know."

"Where is Rosie likely to be?" Quist asked. "Because she is down there somewhere."

"None of her regular people are down there," Davis said. "Her old man dead, Diamond gone, the Bull fired, Hank Benson among the missing. She's looking for someone she knows, I imagine. The night people down there now aren't her people. She's a daytime worker. See you around, Mr. Quist."

Davis disappeared down into his secret labyrinth. Lorch was already on his way to the Stirrup Cup to look for Jerry Carpenter. Quist walked out into the dark night. A few hundred yards away an outside fire flickered. Off to the left a glow of light in the sky indicated that the Stirrup Cup was still doing business. As he walked across the parking lot and onto the stretch of turf leading to the stable area, Quist had the feeling that he was leaving his own world, which he knew well and in which he functioned efficiently, and entering one in which he was familiar with only the most surface routines. The darkness beyond, with only that pinpoint of fire to suggest that there was something focused there, had a sinister feel for Quist. Judith Cameron and Dan had both been the victims of violence there; Willie Jacobs had vanished, been swallowed up; Ed Smythe, whose life was centered there, had stuck his head in a plastic bag and breathed in death. Quist tried to tell himself that the fact that Terry Davis, the undercover security man, hadn't seen Rosie around Shed Row was not significant. Rosie knew every twist and turn of the place, would have been looking for special people, special friends. She'd have had every reason not to advertise her presence. Davis hadn't been looking for her. There was no reason that he must have seen her. But logic didn't help to relieve Quist's feeling of uneasiness. Rosie should have been trying to get in touch with him before this.

Shed Row at the Complex was unlike the stable areas at many of the older tracks, where an original cluster of stalls had been added to and added to, like Topsy "just growed." The design here was planned for the future. There was a main alley with fifty stalls on each side, punctuated by tack rooms for each five stalls. The alley itself was called "Broadway," wide enough for grooming areas outside each stall and for two large feed or trash trucks to operate side by side. There were no uprights to prevent a horse van from backing right up to a box stall door. There were four cross streets, wide as Broadway, each accommodating forty-eight horses, each with its own name—Maple Avenue, East and West; Summer Street, East and West; Grove Street; and Park Avenue. Fully occupied, Shed Row could accommodate just under three hundred horses. There was a water faucet outside each stall. No one had to lug water to any animal for drinking or bathing. A loft area for hay and grain covered each stall. It was a model of efficiency. In the daytime it was splashed with color, alive with constant movement. At night it was dark, silent except for the low whicker of a horse, the stamping of an iron-shod hoof. Shadows moved from place to place, an occasional electric torch winking on and off.

There was something unusual on this particular night and it seemed to have infected the entire place with a feeling of unease. Jerry Carpenter's nine horses—actually eight with the real or ringer King Lear dead and carried away—were stabled on Summer Street East. All the nights before this, Summer Street East had been quiet, dark, with Bull Teliski sitting on a stool outside the tack room. Every fifteen or twenty minutes the ex-prizefighter would move down the line of stalls, checking on the animals he was guarding. The only light in the area came from a little orange button on the Mr. Coffee machine in the tack room behind where the Bull sat on his stool. The Bull was paid to keep things quiet as well as to guard. Horses are the most curious animals; any sounds of activity and they would be up out of their straw, peering over the tops of their box stall doors, talking to each other, stamping. So the Bull would sit there, dreaming of the days when the lights were bright and hot, and he was under them, inside the ropes, taking punishment that he remembered as pleasure. That last time, with Sugar Ray Robinson dancing around him, untouchable, unreachable, flicking away at the scar tissue around the Bull's eyes until the blood came and they stopped it. That was in a gym, sparring. He'd never been good enough for a real match with Sugar Ray. Sometimes, when a fight was being broadcast on radio, the Bull would sit with a battery set on his knees, the sound plugged in to a swollen ear so that only he could hear it. If the action got hot, the Bull's gnarled fists would pantomime punch and counterpunch, his shaved head would duck from side to side.

This night Summer Street East was something else again. Lights were on everywhere: over the stall doors, in the tack room. The Carpenter horses were all up, staring out of their stalls, talking back and forth. The unusual activity had other horses, belonging to other owners in the same block of stalls and in the darkened areas beyond on Summer Street West and up and down Broadway, calling out questions and responses. Five young men wearing ordinary business suits, not stable clothes, were in charge of Carpenter's string.

When other watchmen and stable hands complained of the unusual noise and light, they were advised to "drop dead." An imported radio played loud rock music in the tack room. A watchman for the Dale stable had tried to muscle his way into that tack room to turn off the radio. Kids who just didn't know what they were supposed to do, he thought. That's when the regular inhabitants of Shed Row's night life became aware that Carpenter's new boys were armed and probably ugly enough to use their weapons if pushed.

In another world people disturbed by the neighbors call the cops. There were Lorch's security people to go to. Carpenter, who was responsible for hiring the troublemakers, was only a few hundred yards away at the Stirrup Cup. The Shed Row regulars were not of a mind to ask for help in dealing with muscle. That was the makings of the rumble Terry Davis had reported to Lorch. Shed Row was making up its mind to handle its own problems.

Crossing the turf in the dark toward the flickering fire, Quist knew only what Terry Davis had reported to Lorch. Trouble was brewing, he knew, but not how close it was to explosion. Nor was he familiar enough with routines to know how unusual it was to find a dozen or more men grouped around the fire when he reached it. A babble of conversation that had been going on as he approached was suddenly silenced. Hostility bristled.

"You're Julian Quist, aren't you?" a man on the fringe of the group asked.

Quist made it his business to be seen, to be recognized. "I'm looking for Rosie Wilson," he said. "I dropped her off here awhile back."

Men exchanged looks. It wasn't in the code to give information about any of their own to outsiders. Even though they knew who Quist was, he wasn't one of them.

"She could be in some trouble," Quist said. "I just want to know that she's all right."

"What's the news on Dan Garvey?" someone asked.

"He's making a fight for it," Quist said. "Whoever beat Dan up could have his eye on Rosie."

Dead silence. The flicker of a match as someone lit a cigarette.

"It's possible she knows something that Ed Smythe knew and they want to make sure she doesn't pass it on," Quist said.

"Has she?" a voice asked. Faces were indistinguishable in the darkness, the flicker of light on a cheekbone, a circle of heavy-shoed feet.

"She doesn't know anything to tell," Quist said. "But they don't know that."

"You want to come someplace with me?" a husky voice asked, the voice of a man who had trouble with his vocal cords.

"To do what?" Quist asked.

"Look for Rosie," the voice said.

"If you've got ideas."

"I got ideas," the voice said. The square, hulking figure of a man moved into the circle of light. Face like a battlefield, Lorch had said, flattened nose, scarred upper lip, cauliflower ear.

"You're Bull Teliski?" Quist asked.

"In the flesh."

"I heard you'd been fired."

"Yeah, but this is my place, my people. Being fired doesn't mean I have to go someplace. You want to find Rosie, we can try."

"We need you here, Bull!" a voice cried out.

"Be back—ten minutes," the Bull said. He walked away

into the night and Quist followed. He had to stay almost close enough to touch. Away from the fire the darkness was total.

"You know where Rosie is?" Quist asked.

The Bull turned and closed a powerful hand on Quist's arm. "Just shut up and listen!" he said.

Far away they heard the sound of a car speeding along the deserted thruway. Closer some kind of a night bird made a hooting sound in a treetop. Even closer behind them came the sound of muffled laughter from the crowd around the fire, and the radio music from down the Row.

"Someone could be following us," the Bull said. "Just don't talk till we get where we're goin'. Voices carry."

Quist's sense of direction told him that they were moving in a wide circle that would bring them right back to the stable area only a few yards from where they'd started. The fire around which Bull Teliski's friends huddled was always there, to the right, then behind them, then to the right again.

"You're playing games," Quist whispered.

"Just keep still!" the Bull whispered back.

Quist, aware of a different density of darkness, reached out and found himself touching the wooden wall of a building.

"Rosie!" It was the kind of stage whisper that could be heard from the footlights to the back of the house. There was the squeaking sound of a door moving on a rusty hinge. The mixed aromas of saddle soap and new-mown hay reached Quist, standing only a few feet behind the Bull.

"Rosie!" the Bull tried again. Then he turned to Quist. "Inside," he said.

Quist, a hand touching Teliski's shoulder, followed the ex-fighter through the door, heard it close behind him. A light appeared, made by a torch the Bull was obviously carrying. The cone of light swept the room which was no bigger than a walk-in clothes closet. It was lined with shelves that appeared to be loaded with cans and bottles. There was the door through which they'd come, and another, opposite, that must lead into the main stable area, Quist thought. The light went up and Quist saw a ceiling made of wide planking, wisps of hay showing through the cracks between the boards. On the floor were a couple of horse blankets, spread out as though someone had planned to sleep there. There was a tin coffee mug, half full, on the floor beside the blankets.

"She wasn't supposed to move out of here," the Bull said, turning his light around as though he expected to find Rosie hidden behind the tins of saddle soap and the bottles of liniment on the crowded shelves.

"Why?" Quist asked. It evidently wasn't necessary to whisper here.

"Same reason you gave out there," the Bull said. "Someone may think she knows something they don't want her to tell."

"What 'someone'? Who?" Quist said.

"If I knew that I wouldn't of tried to hide her," the Bull said. "I'd have plowed the sonofabitch under!"

"You like to bring me up to date on what you do know?" Quist asked.

The Bull kept moving his torch around the cramped space, as if he couldn't believe Rosie wasn't hiding somewhere. "Known her since she was five—six years old, and Ed first brought her around the track. Early on I was 'Uncle Bull.' After knowin' her—what, fifteen years?—it was natural she'd come looking for me when she was in trouble."

"She came looking for me yesterday," Quist said.

"I know. She told me. That's why I brought you here, thinkin' she'd be here, where I told her to stay put. We link up in a kind of way, Mr. Quist. Rosie trusts you, and she trusts me. Dan Garvey is a friend of mine, you're his best friend, I understand."

"You know Dan?"

"Sure. He used to come to see me fight, way back. Then when Jerry Carpenter brought his horses out here, we met up again. How bad is he?"

"Bad, but with an outside chance, they think."

"He must have got on to it," the Bull said.

"On to what?" Quist said. "You keep hinting around, Bull, but you don't come out with it."

"Because, for Christ sake, I don't know!" The torch switched off and they were in total darkness again. "You walk into your house or your apartment and you know, without seeing anything out of place, that something's wrong. It's just a feeling you get. Someone's been there, or is in the next room, who shouldn't be there. You look around and you look around and you don't find anything out of place, but something's wrong. You know how that is, Mr. Quist?"

"I've been there," Quist said.

"The day the Carpenter horses got back here from South America it felt wrong. You know what I mean? Five horses they took to South America and five horses they brought back."

"But not the same five?"

The torch was turned, suddenly, full on into Quist's face.

"You talkin' ringer, Mr. Quist?"

"Why not? Everybody else is."

The light went out and Quist tried to blink away the little dots that danced in front of him.

"It wasn't the horses that felt wrong then, it was the people," the Bull said, out of the darkness. "Ed Smythe wasn't himself. You'd think a guy like Ben Diamond, after a trip to a foreign country, would have something to say about it—what he saw there, what he did there. Nothing. Went about his job, talkin' to nobody. It was like him and Ed had some kind of a secret."

"I think they did," Quist said. "I think that secret is why somebody tried to kill Dan."

"Sure it is," the Bull said. "That's why I wanted to hide Rosie away when she came out here, snoopin'. Somebody could think she may know it, too. She told me you thought that, which is why you kept her locked up in your apartment all yesterday."

"Yes."

"Then everything started to go haywire. King Lear, that shouldn't win a plowing contest, sets a new track record. At sixty-to-one there's naturally talk. That night Mr. Carpenter come down here and asked me if I'd keep an eye on Mr. Quigley's horses that are stabled on Grove Street East. His regular watchman was sick, Mr. Carpenter said. Why not? I just had to walk a little way down Shed Row every hour. No big deal. But on that last trip to Grove Street, just before I was due to be relieved, is when Mrs. Cameron was killed. I been in my regular place it would never of happened. Just bad luck, or did someone plan to have me out of there?"

"Carpenter?"

"At least someone knew I would be out of there, off and on."

The Bull wiped the back of his hand across his flattened nose. "And I'm not there tonight!"

"What is going on out there?" Quist asked.

"You know about my kid and his friend? Rosie told me you know about them."

"They followed her from here last night," Quist said. "Parked outside my place waiting for her to show."

"That's not what they say."

"I know what they say," Quist said.

"When the cops called, I said I gave 'em permission to use the stable car. They hadn't asked me, you understand, but if they had I would have told them to go ahead and take it. So lying to the cops was no big deal. But it bothered me, lying to Jerry Carpenter. So this morning when I went off duty I told him. He just laughed, told me he understood. But in the afternoon while I was asleep—I sleep in the daytime, you know—he called me on the phone, said he'd thought it over. Said he was sorry but I was fired. I should pick up a month's pay and that was that. I was real mad at him at first, but then I realized Matt Boylan had persuaded him somehow. My kid had been nosing around Boylan's girl. Anybody named Teliski had to get the axe!"

"Your kid was after Rosemary Wilson," Quist said. "Last night anyway. Maybe he'd been after the Kingman girl some other time, which is why that was the first explanation he thought of when the cops grabbed him. But last night he was after Rosie. Why?"

"I don't know, but if it's true I'll break both his legs when I catch up with him. We don't live together, don't get along. I ain't seen him in a few days."

"But you backed up his story when the police questioned you?"

"What the hell, cops! You defend your own kind against the cops, don't you?" The Bull made a growling sound. "We better stop shooting the breeze and find Rosie."

"You think someone saw you bring her here and grabbed her?"

"Not likely," the Bull said. His torch came on again, focusing on the blankets and the half-full coffee mug. "She's a kid. She heard all that racket outside, not usual. Curiosity got the best of her. We'll find her just outside somewhere."

"I hope," Quist said.

*

Jerry Carpenter, having had a little more than enough to drink, was just getting into his Rolls Royce station wagon outside the Stirrup Cup when Vic Lorch, the Complex security chief, caught up with him.

"Glad I found you before you took off, Mr. Carpenter," Lorch said. "There's something out of order down at your section of Shed Row."

Carpenter steadied himself against the door of the car. "Oh brother!" he said. "What now?"

"The guards you hired to take Teliski's place," Lorch said.

"What do you mean, guards? I hired one man to take over from the Bull."

"There seem to be five or six of them," Lorch said. "Lights on, a lot of shouting back and forth, rock music playing. I'm told they're all armed. The nighttime regulars down there are about to take matters into their own hands. There could be big trouble. I think you could stop it."

"Well, sure," Carpenter said. He sounded vague. He leaned hard on the door of the car. Lorch decided he was really quite drunk.

"Now, Mr. Carpenter," Lorch said.

"Maybe you wouldn't mind driving," Carpenter said. He moved unsteadily around the car to the passenger side.

Lorch got behind the wheel. He needed the key from Carpenter to start the car. As Carpenter fumbled in his pocket for it, Lorch wondered how this one would do driving anywhere, let alone inside the Complex grounds to Shed Row.

"Quite a car," Lorch said, when he got the engine purring.

"Ostentation," Carpenter said. "Rolls-Royce station wagon! Struck me funny."

Lorch wheeled around out of the parking lot. "Where did

these people come from who are guarding your section?" he asked.

"I don't know about 'people,'" Carpenter said. "I went down to Summer Street East this afternoon—yesterday afternoon—to tell Hank Benson, my trainer, that I'd fired Teliski and we'd need a new night watchman. Hank wasn't there. Wasn't a damn soul there. Half a million dollars worth of horse flesh and no one looking out for it, not even an exercise kid. We seemed to be wiped out of people—Smythe dead, Ben Diamond gone somewhere, Hank Benson not paying attention in a sticky situation. I was pretty damn sore. I shell out pretty good money to make sure there are people to look out for my interests."

"So?" Lorch said. The car's headlights focused on the winding dirt road that lead through the woods to the Shed Row buildings.

"I had a couple of friends with me—Juan Ricardo and Matt Boylan. I guess you know them both, don't you, Vic?"

Lorch knew Boylan all too well, an interfering, officious jerk in his opinion. Ricardo he knew no better than to just say "hello" when they passed on the grounds.

"I was up the wall," Carpenter said. "Matt or Johnny Ricardo—I think it was Matt—said he knew a private security firm that could supply me with a night watchman until I found a regular man. Lombard Security, Incorporated. Ever hear of them?"

Lorch had. A reputation for efficiency and for overcharging their customers scandalously. "You got in touch with them?" he asked.

"It was Matt who recommended them," Carpenter said. "I had a business date in the city. Matt said he'd call them for me. I said I'd have Benson here to tell the man they sent what his duties were."

"So you were able to get in touch with Benson?"

"I realized he must be at Aqueduct where I had a horse going and Paul Quigley, for whom Hank also works, had a couple of entries. No way to reach Hank directly, but the switchboard operator promised to get a message to him."

"You talked to him since?"

"Hank? No, but he'd follow orders."

"If he got the message," Lorch said. In Carpenter's world it was obviously unthinkable that messages wouldn't be delivered or orders not followed. You got what you paid for.

The Rolls, quiet as an electric clock, lights dimmed, entered the north end of Broadway in the Row. Horses were up everywhere, staring curiously over the box stall doors. The noise and lights had them all jumpy. They crossed the intersections of Grove Street and Maple Avenue. Summer Street East and West, was next. The blare of the rock music was clearly audible now, lights everywhere.

"What in hell!" Carpenter said.

A man in a dark business suit blocked the turn east into Summer Street. When Lorch stopped the Rolls, the man came around to the driver's side. He had a handgun that was pointed, casually, at the car's passengers.

"You want something?" he asked.

Lorch took a wallet out of his pocket and showed his badge. "Complex Security," he said. "This is Mr. Carpenter, the man you're supposed to be working for. We want to talk to whoever's in charge here."

"You can talk to me," the man said.

"What's going on here?" Carpenter demanded. He seemed to have sobered up.

"No one's permitted to go into this section, that's what's going on," the man said.

"Are you in charge?" Lorch asked.

"Go away, will you, Buster," the man said. "I told you, this section is closed off."

"Like hell it is," Carpenter said. He started to open the door on his side.

The man's gun was suddenly aimed very steadily at him. "Just stay put," the man said, "and drive on. This isn't fun and games, mister."

"I rent this section of Shed Row and I say what goes on here," Carpenter said. But he stopped moving out.

"We got our orders," the man said. "When the head man says we change 'em, we change 'em. And not before. Now keep moving."

You look at a gun in the hand of a creep like that and you pay attention, Lorch thought. "We'll be back in a little," he said. "Tell your head man the orders are changed and he better find out about it, but quick."

The man gave him a crooked smile. "Up yours," he said.

The Rolls moved on quietly down Broadway.

"We let him get away with that?" Carpenter almost shouted.

"When a man has the drop on you, you play it real polite, Mr. Carpenter," Lorch said. "I've got a gun here under my own arm, but there was no way I could reach for it with that guy only two feet away. I've got men I can mobilize in a few minutes. I'll go back, don't worry."

"I just don't understand it," Carpenter said.

"One thing I can tell you, Mr. Carpenter. Lombard Security doesn't send out hoods in tailored suits to guard a stable. They may steal you blind, but they do the job. Somebody else has taken over your territory."

"Who? Why?"

"You got enemies who'd want to damage your horses?" Lorch asked. "You got anything in there beside horses that would interest anybody?"

"No—to both questions!" Carpenter said.

"They've attracted attention on purpose," Lorch said.

"Does that make sense to you? You want to commit a crime, you don't turn on the lights and let the whole damn world know you're up to something."

Rosemary Wilson wasn't "just outside somewhere" as Bull Teliski had predicted. Outside the walls of Shed Row you couldn't see what was going on inside, along Broadway and particularly along the brightly lighted and noisy area of Summer Street East. If Rosie was curious about what was going on, she wasn't to be found wandering around in the outer darkness. Bull Teliski had guided Quist through the inner door of the storage closet where he'd expected to find Rosie into an unused tack room. Crouching there they had witnessed the unusual encounter between Lorch and Carpenter and the man guarding the entrance to Summer Street East. They hadn't been able to hear words, thanks to the noisy rock music, but the gun aimed at the passengers in the station wagon told the story.

"They ain't lettin' Carpenter into his own street," the Bull said in his stage whisper.

"Vic Lorch will be back with his army," Quist said.

"They must know that," the Bull said. "They're like inviting him. How do you figure that?"

"I don't," Quist said. "Where do we look for Rosie?"

"I got to get back to my people," the Bull said. "They plan on comin' down here, gettin' tough with these guys. They don't know about guns."

"Lorch and Carpenter will tell them."

"They ain't headed there," the Bull said. "They'll turn off on Park Avenue and head back to the Security Office. Lorch will have to organize his boys. You want advice, Mr. Quist?"

Quist gave the ex-fighter a tight little smile. "I rarely take it," he said.

"It's your hide," the Bull said. "But I say, go back up to the Security Office yourself. Let Lorch handle this. If there's a shootout you don't want to be in the middle of it. That's what I'm tellin' my people. Let the pros handle it."

"And leave Rosie to be in the middle of it?"

"Look, she's a smart kid, a wise kid, Mr. Quist. She's just slipped into a box stall along the way here. Horses are like people to her. She's gettin' a clear view without anyone seein' her."

"Horses were like people to Judith Cameron," Quist said.

"I don't got time to argue with you, Mr. Quist," the Bull said. "I got to warn my people. Those sonsofbitches on Summer Street could blow their heads off if they come down here to make a stink."

The Bull edged into the storage room, obviously planning to circle back to the fire where his friends were gathered.

Quist stayed in the darkness of the tack room. None of it made any sense to him. Why the lights? Why the raucous music? Why the open show of force against Vic Lorch and Carpenter, both of whom had every right to be on Summer Street East? He didn't know the story of the hiring of the guard, or guards, from Lombard Security. If he had, it still wouldn't have made any sense. Perhaps he should go back to Vic Lorch's office. Rosie might have gone there to find him. That had been their agreement. If she had, Lorch would keep her there. If she hadn't, she was in the middle of what could be big trouble.

Across the way the man who had threatened Lorch and Carpenter was leaning against the door of an end box stall on Summer Street. A horse in the stall suddenly stuck a white-streaked nose out of the open top door and gave the gunman a friendly nudge. The man struck out with his free left hand and struck the horse. The animal let out a squeal of surprise, reared up, and disappeared back into the stall. The gunman moved away out of reach.

Quist went out into the wide alley of Broadway. He stayed in the shadow of the stalls, moving away from the brightly lighted Summer Street crossing.

He called out in a low voice, "Rosie!" He didn't look back at the gunman. He hoped his voice hadn't carried that far. A horse looked out at him, close enough to touch, whinnied a greeting. Perhaps this was someone with feed or sugar or a carrot. Quist forced himself not to look back. Moving away from the gunman he might be allowed to proceed, unquestioned.

A lower stall door swung open just ahead of him.

"In here, Julian!" A tense whisper. It was Rosie.

Quist stepped through the door into the stall, and the girl, crouching in the straw, pulled it closed behind him. In the darkness he heard the low whicker of a horse.

"Don't be afraid of that baby, Julian," Rosie whispered. "He's a lamb. Won't hurt you."

"You should have stayed where Teliski put you," Quist said.

"I couldn't, Julian. All that racket—and where my horses are kept. Did you see what happened to Vic Lorch and Mr. Carpenter?"

"I saw."

"They're crazy people!" Rosie said. "They've never been around a stable before. Do you think Mr. Carpenter hired them to take Bull's place?"

"If he did he didn't know what he was doing," Quist said. "Tell me what's over there on Summer Street."

"Stalls, two tack rooms, two storage rooms for special stuff like liniment, bandages, saddle soap, special gear that isn't used every day. Like hoods with blinders when you're training a horse that's too curious; extra coolers and blankets; tools for working on shoes and hooves if you have an emergency and the blacksmith isn't handy. Poor Ed could shoe a horse better than most blacksmiths. Odds and ends, like extra girths, extra saddle cloths."

"Rooms like the ones where Bull stashed you away."

She nodded and then said, "Yes," aware that he couldn't see her unspoken response in the pitch blackness of the stall.

"If they wanted to steal something, why didn't they just take it and go, instead of letting everyone know they were there?" she asked.

"I don't know. I don't get it," Quist said. "If I hadn't seen that gun and the way it was used, I'd have thought they were just some hopped-up kids raising hell for the fun of it."

"That man over there is no kid, Julian."

"I know."

There was a slamming sound behind him, and Quist turned. The upper half of the box stall door had been shut. He could hear the sliding of metal bolts.

"My God, Julian, someone's locked us in here!" Rosie said. She was on her feet, pounding on the door in the total darkness.

Quist stood very still, his muscles tensed. "There's no point in that, Rosie," he said quietly. "You'll only attract attention from those characters on Summer Street."

"We already have," Rosie said. "Who else would lock up a stall without checking?"

Quist put his shoulder against the door and pushed. It didn't give at all. New building, new hardware, everything snug and solid.

"Window in here?" he asked.

"Two ventilators high up at the back," Rosie said. "Not big enough to crawl through, even if you could rip the screening off them."

"So that appears to be that," Quist said. "When Lorch comes back we'll make him hear us."

She reached for him in the darkness and he felt her small, wiry body clinging to him. "If they come after us?" she whispered.

He reached into the side pocket of his jacket for the small handgun he was carrying. "I may turn out to be a more interesting reception committee than they expect," he said.

Outside the sound of the rock music beat against the night.

On evenings when there was no event at the Arena, Vic Lorch's security force was reduced to a small patrol group. Back at his office a sophisticated push-button dialing system made it possible to alert his people with one spoken message onto a tape.

The one way, Lorch told himself, to deal with a handful of gun-toting spooks was to overwhelm them with numbers. In addition to calling in his own people, he also contacted the State Police and asked for help. A timing was arranged—a half an hour from then—when they could all move in together.

That done, Lorch found a number for Lombard Security and dialed it. "24-hour service" the yellow-page ad announced. A night operator answered his call. Who were the people they had sent out to the Complex and what had their instructions been?

"They stand a chance of being gunned down if I don't have the right answers," Lorch told a half-sleepy voice.

After a few minutes that seemed endless, the Lombard operator came back on.

"You said, 'people,' Mr. Lorch. We sent one man out there, operative Dave Crowther. He was hired by Mr. Henry Benson and he got his detailed instructions from Mr.

Benson. All I have here is that he was employed to act as a night watchman at the stables at the Complex."

"He didn't take other men with him?"

"No indication of it on the employment card here. I have a telephone number for Henry Benson—"

"So have I," Lorch said. He turned to Jerry Carpenter, who was pacing the office, repeated the Lombard report. As he talked, he was dialing the motel where the trainer lived. Again a switchboard operator answered. Benson's room was rung persistently, but there was no answer.

"What are we stalling for?" Carpenter wanted to know.

"So that we go in in force and avoid the risk of being picked off one by one," Lorch said. From a gun rack in the corner he selected a machine pistol and began to check the loading.

"You make a shooting gallery out of Summer Street and there are valuable animals that can be hurt," Carpenter said. "What's to be lost by waiting till daylight?"

"Time," Lorch said.

"At least you could see what you're doing then." Carpenter glanced at his watch. "Going on three o'clock. It'll be light in a couple of hours. I've got a big investment down there, Lorch, and animals I care about."

"Could be we'll take up a position and wait," Lorch said. "Make certain nobody skips out on us," He took a moment to light a cigarette. "The question is, Carpenter, will they wait?"

"To do what?"

"They've got one man, alive or dead, down there," Lorch said. "The fellow Hank Benson hired from Lombard, Dave Crowther. They must have taken over from him, and he certainly wasn't left to run around loose, or he'd have let us know what happened. Quist's down there, Rosemary Wilson. They could walk right into it, not knowing what's up.

My man Davis reported that the regular night people were getting ready to start something. They don't know they're walking into guns. So you see, friend, there are people as well as animals who're in danger down there."

"For God sake, haven't we had enough violence?" Carpenter said. His voice was unsteady. The liquor was wearing off and he was shaken.

"It started with your horse, King Lear. While we're waiting for men, why don't you level with me about that, Carpenter?"

"Level? There's nothing to level about," Carpenter said. He sounded shrill.

"Where did you find a ringer that could pass for King Lear?" Lorch asked. He was an old hand at question-and-answer. He knew when he'd touched a sore spot.

"The horse had the breeding for speed," Carpenter said. "By Bulldozer and Desert Flower. He just came alive, that's all."

"Mrs. Cameron knew you'd pulled a fast one, and she checked on it."

"No!"

"It was a joke that got serious, right? When she found you out, you knew you'd be barred from racing for life, be hit with a criminal charge. I don't think you, personally, killed the lady or tortured the horse, but someone who was in on it with you did. Was it Ed Smythe?"

"You're dreaming!" Carpenter said.

"So you try dreaming," Lorch said. "What other reason could there possibly have been for what happened?"

"I wish to God I knew!" Carpenter cried out. "Judith was my friend, a dear friend, a close friend."

The office door opened and two men in work clothes came in. The first of the reinforcements had arrived. Lorch picked up the machine pistol.

"We'll talk about this again, Carpenter," he said. "We'll talk about it a lot more, later."

"State troopers are coming in without lights or sirens," one of the new arrivals reported.

"Let's go," Lorch said. "And don't take time to ask too many questions. Those bastards down there are trigger happy."

3

Quist and Rosie Wilson stood pressed against the door of the box stall where they were imprisoned, trying to hear what was going on outside. The music from Summer Street was loud. That appeared to be all; no voices, no sound of any special activity.

"Why?" Rosie asked. "Why would they lock us in here?"

"Something's about to happen," Quist said. "We'd have seen it. There's nothing we can do but wait till we hear someone out there who sounds like a friend." He reached out and touched the girl, and she was instantly clinging to him again.

"That man with the gun—he'll use it if they try to cross him," she said.

"I know. So does Lorch. That's why he drove away without putting up a fight. He'll be back, with the odds tilted a little more his way."

"He doesn't know we're here!"

"He knows we're here somewhere," Quist said. "So we wait till he comes back, and then we beat the hell out of this door."

Her fingers tightened on his arm. "It's scary to be locked in like this."

He tightened an arm reassuringly around her. "It won't be long," he said. "You haven't told me what happened after you left me and came here to Shed Row."

"It wasn't like any other time I can remember," she said. "Everybody on edge, the lights and the music down here at Summer Street. Bull Teliski was there, kind of the center of things. Everybody figured he got a raw deal from Mr. Carpenter. Then hiring these noisy jerks down here to take his place. Others that had horses to watch were sore because over two hundred animals were jumpy and nervous. Not one of them was going to be worth a damn today after churning around all night. This one in here was all lathered up when I slipped in with him. He calmed down with someone here. But there aren't enough people to deal with them all. People in this world, Julian, spend their lives trying to keep horses cool, ready for the big effort. Disturbances like this just don't happen. If—if you were trying to guard a bank, noise and lights might keep a thief away. When you're guarding horses, quiet and rest is what you try for."

"I understand there are five or six guys out there," Quist said. "One of Lorch's men reported to him while I was in his office."

"It doesn't make sense," Rosie said. "Ordinarily there would just be Bull, sitting on his stool, quiet, not moving around much. The horses know he belongs there, don't pay any attention to him."

"So that's all your people were talking about? The raw deal Bull got and the noise down here on Summer Street?"

"Till I joined them," Rosie said. "Then there were a lot of questions about Ed Smythe. I hadn't seen any of those people since Ed was found."

"And you told them what you told me? About his being drunk and his talk of a sellout and big money?"

"No! You scared me out of that, Julian. Someone there could have been anxious to learn how much I know. I told them that Ed seemed different when he got back from South America a few days ago. This got everyone talking about the possibility of King Lear being a ringer. There was talk about Ben Diamond and where he may have gone."

"Where?"

"No one knows. No one even knows where he came from originally."

"They tie him in to what happened to Dan Garvey?"

"Some do," Rosie said. "They think Mr. Garvey may have pressured Ben, not believed his story. Ben, determined to get away from him and from the police, struck him down. When he thought he'd killed him, he borrowed somebody's truck and took him away. Didn't want the body found here."

"But left it on a city street where the first patrol car would spot it. Whose truck? Do they know whose truck it was?"

"No one seems to. There are half a dozen pickups around with Connecticut plates. No one's reported one missing or stolen."

"Did anyone mention Willie Jacobs?"

"No. I mean, it was mentioned that you and Willie found Ed in his garage, but no one mentioned Willie not being around. This isn't Willie's regular stamping ground, you know. He's usually where the horses are racing—Aqueduct this week, Saratoga next week. He follows the running, not the stable care or the training. Not seeing him around here wouldn't mean to any of my people that he's missing. It wasn't talked about."

"He wouldn't have stayed out of touch if he could have helped it," Quist said.

"Julian!" The girl's fingernails bit through the sleeve of his jacket. "Smell!"

"Smell what?"

"Smoke!" the girl cried out. "Oh my God, Julian! There's a fire up in the loft!"

He looked up. Through the wide cracks in the floorboards he saw a small flicker of flame. The horse, behind them in the darkness, whickered nervously.

At the same moment the music from Summer Street was drowned out by the full-throated wail of a siren. Voices were shouting.

Rosie began pounding on the locked stall door, screaming for help. She had barely begun when Quist heard the sound of the door bolts being slid free! The stall door opened, and Quist found himself confronted by a wall of flame across the alley in Summer Street. People were running from everywhere.

"Better step on it, Julian," a familiar voice said.

It was Willie Jacobs who had set them free.

The main focus of the fire was on Summer Street. Quist didn't have time to think about it, but the fire in the loft above the stall in which he and Rosie had been locked must have been separately started, designed to burn the prisoners to a crisp.

What looked like a toy fire engine, belonging to the Complex, barreled down Broadway toward the blaze. A horse running free, eyes bulging, ran down a would-be fire fighter and left him writhing on the ground.

Quist found himself frozen where he stood. Willie Jacobs was pulling at his arm. Rosie Wilson had reacted in a way he should have expected. Horses were her life. She had torn off the sweater she was wearing and gone back into the stall where the horse who had been their co-prisoner stood shuddering. She tied the sweater over the animal's eyes and, talking softly to him, led him out onto Broadway. Horses, Quist remembered, would run back into a burning stable because their stalls represented safety to them.

Instinctively Quist started to move toward Summer Street, the center of the action.

"Don't go, Julian," Willie said. "That's what you're supposed to do."

"What are you talking about?" Quist looked down at Willie. The little man, usually so dapper, looked as though he had slept in his clothes, and he badly needed a shave.

"Look," Willie said. "Everybody running there. The night workers, the cops, the security guards. This fire isn't what you call spontaneous combustion, Julian. It was set different places because that's where they want people to go, except the one here. That was set to polish off you and Rosie. I saw."

"You *saw* someone start the fire?"

"The goon that was guarding Summer Street over there, the one who was waving a gun around under Vic Lorch's nose. The one who slipped across Broadway and locked you and Rosie in. He climbed up the outside ladder and torched the hay over your heads."

"Can you point him out?"

"If I see him again. Julian, let's get out of here and see if we can make sense."

"Where were you, Willie?"

"Would you believe in the loft right above you? When that bastard came up and held his lighter to the hay he was looking right at me, but he didn't see me in the dark. I'm a man who's been hiding since yesterday."

"Why?"

"Someone saw Rosie talking to me, followed her to you

where I sent her. I was as good as dead unless I got the goods on someone. When all this racket started down here, I needed a place to watch. Turned out to be right over the stall they shut you in. I tried to smother the fire but it spread too fast."

More horses were being led out of the fiery area across the way. A town fire engine, siren screaming, came down Broadway, scattering horses and the men trying to rescue them.

"I tell you, Julian, those fires were started deliberately," Willie insisted. "They want everybody rushing in here. That means something is happening somewhere else. You see what I mean?"

What Willie was trying to say began to percolate in Quist's head. Everybody on the Complex lot was here, or was headed here: cops, security people, night shift people. Nothing else that was normally watched, no area that was normally patrolled, was being cared for now. Hundred of thousands of dollars in horses and property were being threatened, and every able-bodied person within range was centered here, trying to help keep down the size of the disaster. Grove Street, Maple Avenue, Park Avenue, and the north and south ends of Broadway were unwatched. Ten-to-one the guards who were posted at the entrance gates to the Complex had left their posts and were here or on their way here.

"What is it, Willie?" Quist asked. "You have any idea what they're up to?"

"Rosie told you what Ed Smythe told her. I sent her to tell you," Willie said. "Forty-odd million dollars of drugs, street value! What do a few dead horses and a few dead men and a few burned-out buildings matter if you're after that kind of loot?"

*

The confusion on Summer Street was beyond belief: people shouting, animals screaming. A chestnut filly, her tail on fire, raced up and down the crowded alley, scattering would-be fire fighters. Some animals were led quietly out of their stalls, following dogs or goats. Others reared up and slashed out at potential rescuers. The night force of people who knew anything about handling horses was less than a quarter of the number who would have been there in the daytime. The holocaust had sprung into being in a matter of minutes with no chance to alert experienced help living in the distant village or in the boardinghouses scattered over the countryside. Men with the best of intentions tried to handle animals who refused to be handled. Panic was the name of the game.

Vic Lorch, sweat running down his pale, angry face, was looking for one man, the man with the gun who had driven him off half an hour before the disaster began. In the crowd of fire fighters and horse people trying desperately to rescue terrified animals, it was almost impossible to recognize faces in the flickering light from the flames. Lorch, elbowing his way through the disorganized crowd, climbing over tangled hoses, was trying also to locate Terry Davis, his undercover operator. Davis could undoubtedly identify the gunman and the others who had been with him. But no Davis. He could be in one of those burning stalls trying to help.

Lorch came face-to-face with Jerry Carpenter. The millionaire owner appeared to be in shock, tears streaming, looking at Lorch as though he was a complete stranger.

"My God, my God, my God!" he kept muttering over and over. He pushed on past Lorch, as if something of vital importance waited for him somewhere away from the flames, the shouting, the screaming animals. A man in a trance.

It was then that Lorch saw Rosie Wilson running along the

row of burning stalls on the south side of Summer Street. He shouted at her, hoping she could tell him where Quist might be. If she heard him, which was unlikely in all the noise, she paid no attention. He saw her dart into one of the stalls. In the loft overhead fire raged. Damn fool kid, he thought, and wedged his way through a group of fire fighters playing a feeble stream of water in the general direction of the flames. He had just reached the stall into which Rosie had disappeared when she came out, leading a horse with a blanket thrown over its head. She was coughing and choking.

"There's a man in there," she said to Lorch. "Unconscious. I had to get Clothilda out. She—she's my horse. Poor baby—she's burned in a dozen places. Stuff falling through from the loft." She stroked Clothilda's sweat-streaked face. "Easy, darlin'. I'll have you out of here in no time." She led the frightened animal toward the relative quiet of Broadway.

"Quist?" Lorch shouted after her.

"He was all right a few minutes ago," she called back. "Willie Jacobs is with him."

Lorch took a deep breath and charged into the stall the girl had just vacated. Fire was dropping through the planking from the loft overhead. The straw on the floor of the stall was burning in spots. He saw the body of a man, clothes on fire. He grabbed the man under the arms and dragged him out into the clear. He took off his own coat and tried to smother the fire that was burning the man's clothes. Looking down, he noticed that his hands were covered with blood.

The man was obviously dead, his head beaten in. Lorch felt inside the man's smoking jacket and found a wallet. Inside it was an I.D. card. "David Crowther, Lombard Security." This was the man who had been sent to take Bull

Teliski's place. He felt no pain from the fire. He was dead long before it started.

There were other things to be saved from the fire beside valuable horseflesh. The tack rooms along burning Summer Street were filled with valuable gear: racing saddles, training saddles, bridles, blankets, coolers, blinker hoods, special equipment used for special purposes on special horses. Men who worked the stables and saw their horses led to safety, or left to roast alive in the burning stalls, thought of the irreplaceable gear and fought their way into the tack rooms to get out what they could. Some of it was just thrown into the alley, getting in the way of fire fighters, creating stumbling blocks for men and horses. Cooler heads were using the rear exits, like the one Bull Teliski had used as a hiding place for Rosie. Some men had actually produced pickup trucks and cars into which to load the stuff they retrieved.

Circulating away from the core of the fire, not quite certain what they were looking for, Quist and Willie Jacobs saw some of this gear being carried out and loaded from the outer rim of burning Summer Street.

"Like saving your toothbrush after all your teeth have been pulled," Willie muttered. Then his hand closed on Quist's wrist like a vise. "Holy cow, Julian! That pickup backed up in the center there—fellow with the black cap pulled down over his forehead!"

"What about him?"

"That's Ben Diamond, Carpenter's stableman," Willie said. "Guy you were looking for. Guy who paid for his room and took off—with something under a tarpaulin in the back of his truck."

The man who had shot King Lear—or King Lear's double.

The man who had fired a stray bullet that had lodged in Judith Cameron's brain—or who had killed her deliberately. The man who may have left Garvey for dead in the back of a truck on the waterfront. He stood by the tailgate of the pickup. Other men, city-dressed men, were bringing stuff out of the tack room. Diamond seemed to check each item before they tossed it into the truck. One or two things were discarded and thrown away into the grass.

"Those other creeps are the ones who were guarding Carpenter's horses earlier," Willie said. "I'd know them anywhere."

Quist felt his jaw muscles tighten. "See if you can find Vic Lorch, Willie," he said. "He must be around front somewhere. Tell him what's here. And quick, Willie. It can't take forever for them to load what they're after."

Willie slipped away toward the din of Summer Street. The distance between Quist and the truck being loaded by Diamond and his friends was not more than fifty yards. On the outside of Shed Row there was elaborate planting—forsythia, lilac. If Diamond's attention wasn't attracted, there might be a way to get close to him by moving from bush to bush. Quist wanted to get his hands on Diamond more than he had ever wanted anything in his whole life. Like a flashback in a movie he was seeing Dan Garvey's grey face on the operating table, doctors bending over him. He could hear Dr. Thomas's voice: "*They beat the hell out of your friend.*" Diamond, Quist told himself. Diamond, driving Dan into the city, hidden under that tarpaulin. Diamond, leaving Dan to die because he believed he was already dead. Diamond, who like Ed Smythe had had his price but could live with it.

Quist moved in the shadows, a few yards closer, pausing behind a forsythia bush. He had taken his gun out of his pocket. The palm of his hand was sweating. He had never deliberately shot a man in his life, but if he had to, Diamond was it.

The city-dressed men came out of the tack room carrying some gear. They dumped it into the back of the truck. These men were armed, Quist knew. He recognized the Summer Street guard who had driven off Vic Lorch a little earlier, had, according to Willie, locked him and Rosie in that stall across the way and set fire to the hay in the loft above them.

"That's the lot," Quist heard one of the men say.

"So let's get the hell out of here," another said.

There were five men in addition to Diamond. Three climbed into the body of the truck with the gear. Diamond stood aside to let the other two get into the cab of the truck. He would obviously join them, probably to guide them safely out of the Complex grounds.

Quist moved, faster than he could ever remember moving before in his life. They had to see him coming. Someone shouted a warning. A gun flashed and then another. Quist reached Diamond, who was just climbing into the cab, wrenched him free, and went rolling away across the grass, fighting to keep Diamond's arms pinioned at his sides. There were more shots and Quist felt a sudden, searing pain in his left shoulder.

The truck was moving fast, rocking its way down the grade toward the south end of Shed Row. Diamond's friends were not stopping to rescue him. Quist looked down into a face, twisted with fear, and drove his right fist with every ounce of strength he had into a mouth that opened to cry out.

Diamond was suddenly still. Quist rolled away to one side, gasping for breath. He reached up to touch the agony in his left shoulder, and his hand came away bloodied. He reached out, grabbed at Diamond's long, dark hair, and yanked him into a sitting position.

Diamond's eyes were blurred, unfocused.

"You and I have some talking to do, chum," Quist said. "We can do it here and now, or I'll take you somewhere I can carve it out of you."

"Quist! Are you all right?" Someone was running across the turf from Broadway. In the sudden flare-up from the burning barn behind him, Quist saw that it was Juan Ricardo, Jerry Carpenter's South American friend. He was suddenly kneeling in the grass beside Quist and Diamond. "My God, Quist, I was just coming from the Stirrup Cup when I saw you take out after this fellow, rip him off the truck. The gunfire stopped me for a moment. What on earth—?"

Quist let go of Diamond, and the stable hand dropped back onto the grass, moaning.

"Friend of mine has gone for the security people," Quist said, still trying to catch his breath. "This is Ben Diamond. I think he may have murdered Mrs. Cameron, tried to murder Dan Garvey. Those friends of his who took off in the truck set that fire. I got lucky, or Rosemary Wilson and I would have been cooked to a turn."

"You're hurt," Ricardo said. "Bleeding."

"One of them winged me."

"What were those people after?" Ricardo asked. "They seemed to have a truckload of stuff."

"It looked like stable equipment," Quist said. "Saddles, blankets, God knows what else. Our friend here is going to tell us when he comes to."

"Vandals!" Ricardo said. "Horses, people, property—all for some tack room gear."

"You have horses up there?" Quist asked.

"Fortunately north on Grove Street," Ricardo said. "They seem to have pretty well isolated the fire to Summer Street East. What can I do to help you?"

Quist clutched at his shoulder. "Just stay with me till Willie Jacobs shows up with some security people."

"Let me see what I can do to stop that bleeding," Ricardo said. "Can you take off your jacket?"

The effort was excruciating. Quist realized that somewhere between the place where he'd pulled Diamond off the truck and the spot they'd rolled to he'd lost his gun. Sounds from the disaster area seemed to blend together, echo. Someone was telling him about a ship intercepted by the Coast Guard carrying drugs stored away in automobile tires. "*Weighing no more than two defensive tackles on the Dallas Cowboys.*"

"A light load for a pickup truck," Quist said.

"Just be still, Quist," Ricardo said. He was tearing Quist's black knit shirt from the wound. "There! Nasty business." From far away Ricardo's slightly accented voice said something about a doctor

He came to in what seemed like waves, circular waves of returning consciousness. He'd obviously fainted from the pain. He couldn't feel anything in the shoulder area now. He reached up with his right hand and found that he was heavily bandaged, his arm immobilized by some kind of cast.

There were voices at some distance from him. He opened his eyes and found himself staring up at a white ceiling. There was an emergency medical facility in the Arena Building at the Complex. He guessed that's where he was, in a small private room. He turned his head toward the voices he'd heard.

There was a doctor in a green hospital gown. With him was Juan Ricardo, his white sharkskin suit grass stained. They saw Quist move and came over to the bed on which he was lying.

"Feeling better? Bullet broke your arm just below the shoulder joint, Mr. Quist. I'm Dr. Prosser. You fainted from the pain. When Mr. Ricardo got you here, I put you out solidly while I got you tacked together again. You'll be carrying your arm in a sling for a while, but nothing permanent."

"How soon can I get out of here?" Quist asked.

"Couple of hours, when the effects of the anaesthetic have completely worn off. If you'll excuse me, we're flooded with patients—major and minor burns."

"How are things at Shed Row?" Quist asked.

"The fire appears to be under control," Ricardo said. The doctor had gone. "The cost, animal and human—?" He shrugged expressive shoulders.

"Ben Diamond?"

"I regret to say, Quist, that he—he may have gotten away."

"My God, man!"

"It was a choice I had to make," Ricardo said. "Sitting on him, or getting you to where you could get proper help. He was still lying there in the grass when I carried you to my car and brought you here."

"I should be grateful," Quist said. "But that bastard has all the answers."

"You could have bled to death," Ricardo said. "Your security men didn't come. I had to make a choice."

"Again, I should be grateful. But I was so damn close."

Ricardo's bright eyes fixed on Quist. "Close to what, my friend?"

"I think I told you out there. The murder of Mrs. Cameron, the attempt to murder Dan Garvey. Diamond is it, or knows who it is."

"That's all?" Ricardo asked.

"Isn't that enough?"

"Those other men in the pickup. You think they set a fire just to steal a few hundred dollars worth of stable gear?" Ricardo asked.

The inside of Quist's mouth felt dry. Suddenly it all seemed dangerously clear to him. What was it Jerry Carpenter had said about Juan Ricardo? "*A horse nut. It was through his urging I sent a string of horses to South America.*" And streetwise Mike Romano, the manager of the Stirrup Cup? "*Two hundred kilos is worth forty million. But you don't need the United States Navy to bring it in. We're talking about five pounds of powder.*" A freighter, flying a Greek flag, with the drugs stashed away in automobile tires. What about half a dozen horses flown in from South America, the valuable powder sewn into the linings of saddles, of blankets, in bottles and cans labeled as animal vitamins? Five hundred pounds of added weight in such a cargo would scarcely be noticed. The cooperation of Ed Smythe and Ben Diamond would have made it child's play to get the contraband at least as far as Shed Row at the Complex. After that something had gone wrong with the distribution of the drugs to the street market. What was it Kreevich always said? The man who pulls the trigger isn't always the real villain, but the man who pays to get it done.

Ricardo was smiling down at him. Quist had the uncomfortable feeling that those bright eyes were reading his mind.

"So Ed Smythe did talk to his daughter and she carried the word to you," Ricardo said very quietly. He took his hand out of his jacket pocket, and in his palm was Quist's little handgun. "You dropped this in the grass when you pulled Diamond off that truck." He slipped it back into his own pocket. "I could have finished you off out there, Mr. Quist, but it seemed to me there was a chance you might be willing to deal."

"For money?"

"For your life," Ricardo said. "The lives of people you care for. You think one policeman in the hospital could save Garvey and Miss Morton if we chose to get to them? People have fumbled this deal, jeopardized it beyond belief. But I don't choose to pay the piper—as they say."

"What do I have to deal with?" Quist asked.

"How much you know, with whom you've shared it," Ricardo said.

"And after I tell you that, what chance do I have?" Quist asked.

"My dear man, you don't have any chance at all as things appear to stand," Ricardo said. "If Ed Smythe told his Rosemary all he knew, and she passed it on to you, and you have already told the police, none of us is going to survive. Somehow I don't think that can be, or the police would have been swarming down on us long ago. So what I do in the next hour depends on how much you know and who else knows it."

"You claim you knew Ed Smythe well," Quist said. "Do you honestly believe he would have told his daughter anything that would place her in danger?"

"A man who has made up his mind to take his own life may tell anyone anything," Ricardo said. "You know what those men were taking away in that truck, don't you?"

"Stable gear, worth a few hundred dollars," Quist said.

Ricardo shook his head, slowly, from side to side, "I'm afraid that won't do, Mr. Quist. Either Ed Smythe told you or you have guessed. Which is it?" He glanced at his gold wristwatch. "Your friend Garvey stumbled on the truth and he hasn't been able to talk so far. You have guessed. It doesn't really matter as far as the contents of the truck is concerned. It should be long gone to a safe place by now. What matters are names. Did Smythe give his daughter names?"

"You've blown it, haven't you, as far as you're concerned?" Quist said.

"I'll be long gone, out of the country, within the next hour," Ricardo said. "Regretfully, but untouchable. But the names of others, Mr. Quist. Did Smythe give his daughter other names?"

"Like Matthew Boylan?" a voice from the doorway asked.

Ricardo spun around to find himself facing Lieutenant Kreevich of Manhattan Homicide. Kreevich, his face stony, was aiming a service revolver directly at Ricardo's heart.

" 'Fumble' is a word you used, Ricardo," Kreevich said. "Oh brother, have you fumbled!"

Behind Kreevich in the doorway of the little private room were Vic Lorch and two of his men. Almost before Ricardo could react, his wrists were handcuffed behind his back and Kreevich had gone over him and produced a gun of his own plus Quist's little weapon from his side pocket.

"The truck didn't make it," Kreevich said. "Vic's men didn't fall for the bait. They stayed at their posts at the gates. When your people tried to shoot their way out, Ricardo, it cost them."

Quist, propped up on an elbow, asked one question. "Diamond?"

"Dead," Kreevich said. "I have a feeling Ricardo polished him off before he brought you up here. Diamond was probably ready to talk."

"How did you know I was here?" Quist asked.

"Your friend Willie Jacobs saw Ricardo lug you up here," Kreevich said. "I was here because, I'm happy to tell you, Dan Garvey spoke a word."

"A word?"

"One word—Boylan." Kreevich's smile was mirthless.

"When I got here all hell had broken loose. With everybody fighting the fire, I had trouble finding Vic. But Willie spotted me, told me about you and Diamond and the truck and Ricardo, the Good Samaritan who wanted you to talk before he polished you off. One of your fumbles, Ricardo. Julian didn't have any names to give you. I wonder how far you'll go in the matter of names to save a part of your own hide?"

It seemed like years ago, not just a few hours. Quist was sitting in his own wicker armchair, on his own terrace, at his own apartment on Beekman Place. His own woman sat beside him, her cool hand resting on his. His own Jack Daniels on the rocks was nectar. Violence was something far away, his own world being pieced together once more. Garvey, in the hospital, had spoken only one word, a name, but his vital signs were good.

Mark Kreevich sat facing his friends, looking exhausted but pleasantly relaxed.

"Once he started talking, Ricardo couldn't stop," Kreevich said. "A grim comedy of errors. My God, when you think of the people who are dead or hurt, the horses, the property!"

"With forty-odd million dollars dangling in front of them," Lydia said.

"The men really behind it are as elusive as God," Kreevich said. "The Syndicate, the Mafia, whatever you choose to call them. An army out for criminal profit that fouls up our lives in so many areas. The one person we've nailed of consequence is Matthew Boylan. An apparent socialite, a home in Connecticut, another in Florida, an investor in the Complex. So much of his criminal world could be played safely in front of that phony backdrop. Drugs, we have to believe, was the main game. Ricardo, you might say, was a kind of stage manager, whose special job was to keep people looking the other way. A South American playboy sharing caviar and champagne with the super-rich Americans. Boylan and Ricardo were behind the hundreds of small airfields used to bring in drugs in relatively small quantities. There was a sudden demand for a big delivery, street customers not getting what they needed. Horses were Ricardo's special sideline, special pleasure. His mind gravitated that way, and he saw the possibility of bringing in a few hundred kilos with a shipment of horses. If someone here would send down horses for a race meeting in Buenos Aires, no one would pay any particular attention when the time came to ship them back. Jerry Carpenter was Ricardo's sucker for that plan. He sent down some second-rate horses, including King Lear. When the time came to load them for the return trip, with two hundred kilos of heroin stashed away in the gear, King Lear fell when he was being loaded on a truck to take him to the airport. Broke a leg and had to be destroyed. If they were short a horse, it might lead to inquiries. You understand, Ed Smythe and Ben Diamond had been offered enough money to dazzle them forever.

"Now, by coincidence, the great stallion Bulldozer had been engaged by some South American horseman to stand at stud down there, service a dozen or so brood mares. One of those mares was owned by Ricardo, and the resulting foal was a dead ringer for King Lear. He had no lip tattoo so it was easy to copy King Lear's. No one would notice that it was a fresh mark and not two years old as it should have been. After all, they only planned to substitute him for the trip, not to race him. That's where the grim comedy began. It was all to be so simple. The horse would be brought to the Complex and in a day or two the drugs would be peacefully carried away to the market. But the day they got back, Jerry Carpenter insisted that King Lear be entered in a race at

Aqueduct. Smythe panicked. He could have reported the horse wasn't fit, but rather than make an issue of it that might result in uncomfortable questions, he let the ringer run."

"Result, a track record," Quist said.

"And much talk," Kreevich said. "Worst of all, Judith Cameron suspected something. She stopped at Shed Row to look at the horse she'd raised, and spotted the animal as a phony. Ben Diamond discovered her, argued with her, knocked her out there in the stall. Then he went through the charade of torturing the horse, shooting it, and making sure Judith was done for by firing a shot into her head. Result: police, an investigation. The drugs couldn't be moved in that climate. They were overrun by State Police, Vic Lorch's men, you and Garvey. Any unusual movement of trucks or equipment could produce danger. Carpenter's section of Shed Row was the center of the action. They couldn't get into the tack rooms to unpack the drugs and take them out in small quantities.

"Meanwhile, realizing that he was indirectly responsible for Judith's murder, Smythe got himself blind drunk and said just a little too much to Rosemary. Now two of the people working for Ricardo and Boylan were Bull Teliski's son Peter and Pat Grogan. They spotted Rosemary talking to Willie Jacobs, followed her to town. Not clever boys. They were picked up and concocted the best story they could think of. Once more security tightened around Carpenter's segment of Shed Row.

"How to get people away from the area so they could quietly move the drugs? No way. The flamboyant Mr. Ricardo came up with a stroke of genius, he thought. Instead of isolating Carpenter's area, he'd bring everybody to it. Carpenter was pressured by Boylan to fire Bull Teliski. Crowther, the man sent by Lombard Security, was done away with, and Ricardo's people took over. They staged a noisy rock session, causing all the regulars to get together to come up with a way to stop them. Then the fire. No one would be doing anything then but trying to save horses and property. In the confusion they would truck away the gear in which the drugs were hidden. Ben Diamond was there to identify what things to take. But the fumbles went on. First there was Vic Lorch with Carpenter, trying to put a stop to things before they were quite ready. There was you and Rosemary, Julian, snooping around. Finally, when the holocaust was underway, one thing they had counted on didn't happen. The security men at the gates didn't leave their posts to fight the fire. When a truck tried to leave, there was a logical question to ask: why would anyone be leaving when they were needed in an emergency? The answer was guns. The final fumble. Two of the five men were shot and killed, the other three threw in the towel."

Kreevich held out his empty glass to Lydia. "One of the dead ones is Peter Teliski, the Bull's son. Grogan surrendered with two others. You didn't know them by sight, so you didn't recognize them on the truck, Julian."

"You've left Dan out of this," Quist said.

"Ricardo says that Dan, searching around Carpenter's stables, obviously for some clue to Judith's murder, found some of the heroin. Diamond came up behind him and killed him, he thought, with a blacksmith's hammer. He backed a pickup truck to the tack room and loaded what he thought was a dead body. Where to take it? What to do with it? The truck was Boylan's, Connecticut plates. He drove it into the city, took the plates off, and left it. We'll know when Dan comes around."

"So many good people, so many great horses," Lydia said.

Kreevich smiled, a genuine smile, the smile of a man who

wants to forget for a moment what's behind him. "I mentioned the tragedy of so many great horses being burned alive or permanently damaged to your friend Willie Jacobs. He said you don't call a horse 'great' till it can match up with a famous filly in the old days in Kentucky. That filly was so fast, Willie says, that she stopped on the backstretch of a race, dropped a foal, and still won the race."

"Oh, come on!" Lydia said.

Kreevich laughed. "According to Willie, the foal finished second!"